"A 'must-have' for any collector of great fiction. T. Cass has masterfully captured the tales of Sampson and Jaslyn...It is as though you know them personally."

Millicent Courtney-Ware, author of ***The Freak Within***

"I laughed out loud...the whole story was engaging, sensual, funny, sweet, and downright good. I love the characters and I want to learn more about them."

Misty Tippen, Owner of Enchanted Events

"A charming, funny look at love and the many obstacles we face when we've found it."

J. Monique Gambles, author of ***When the Drama Has Ceased***

"***Labor of Love*** was an honest look at how emotions are thrust into the reality of life. T. Cass does a wonderful job in expressing the impact of family and friends in our search for love. But though the up and downs, good and bad, she shows us that we can find exactly what we are looking for, and that's love. I thoroughly enjoyed reading about the journey that we all will, at one time, will take."

B. K. Pope, M. Ed.

Labor of Love

By T. Cass

Ivy Pyramid Publishing

ISBN: 0-9764634-1-5

Published by Ivy Pyramid Publishing
P.O. Box 11524
Fort Worth, TX. 76110

Library of Congress Control Number: 2005920960

Cover Concept: Patricia Cass
Cover Design & Logo: Kaos Factor Design Concepts

Poetry written by T. Cass

Dedication

For Sarah and Patricia, my past.
You give me courage.

For Michelle, Cassandra, and Adrianne, my present.
You give me strength.

For Jasmine and Ashlyn, my future.
You give me inspiration.

Prologue

I've often heard it said that men are from Mars, and women hover somewhere around Venus. That's bullshit! This statement implies that men and women think differently, and that is not the case. We're all from the same planet…Earth. We just have some fucked up ways of thinking about love. Men are too busy worried about the first and only love who broke their hearts, and women are too busy concentrating on finding the love of their lives. As a protective measure, both sexes do the opposite of what they probably should do–they both run from what could be perceived as the inevitable. Falling in love.

When a man does meet a good woman, he starts having flashbacks of the first girl that broke his heart, so he does something stupid to mess up the current relationship. This self-fulfilling prophecy only helps to prove his own jacked up theory–relationships aren't worth the trouble. His statement, "I just want to keep my life as uncomplicated as possible."

Women, on the other hand, begin to hold on too tight. Thinking that this may be THE ONE, they start sacrificing all sorts of time and energy on a dude they haven't known for a good forty-five minutes. As soon as they meet, it's already like "Hmm, we'll go here, and we'll go there. I think I want him to meet my mama. I guess they'll meet when we go to church on Sunday." Shit! What brother wouldn't run? And fast!!! The funny thing is that most women don't even realize that this willingness to please a man so badly does not originate from a desire to be loved, but it starts from a fear of commitment. As she squeezes harder and harder, she's not saying, "I love you." She's really saying how much do I have to smother you or get on your nerves before you've had enough and leave me? When he does leave, her theory has been proven right, yet again.

If you don't believe me, then just watch a man that's in a relationship with a woman who's willing to cook, clean, and give him a little booty on a regular basis. Watch. Just watch and tell me he's actually satisfied because he'll find something wrong, or, he'll find every reason in the book to kick it with his boys–everyday! *Or*, he may start going out to the club, coming in late, or he may simply neglect his girl to the point that she starts to nag his ass under the pressure of trying to keep him. When that happens, it's over! Old girl can forget those dreams of the two-story with the white picket fence 'cause brotherman is on his way out the door. The speech goes something like this: "I'm suffocating in this relationship. You're too clingy. I need my space." And finally, the coup de grâce, "Let's just see other people."

Watch a sister who meets a man who has a good job, who goes to church on Sunday, and is willing to call her back when she pages him. Those three kids, ex-wife, and baby mama don't matter. "Everybody has kids these days," she says. That criminal record doesn't matter. "That was way last year. He has a decent job now, and he don't have to do that no more. He tryin' to change." This is said with a straight face mind you. Finally, "I know we just met two months ago, but I trust you! That's why I don't mind you staying here until your apartment comes through. We're in this together 'cause I love you, Boo!" Then, when "Mr. Wrong" starts to spend up all her money, freeload, and cheat, her homegirls have to come in and talk some sense into her ass when she's sitting up broke, busted, and disgusted.

He's gone! She's gone! That's what the story should have been called. It's like we're both so busy running we wind up missing each other and the love we need because we're looking or running too hard. Some of us will even lie and say we're not looking for love or a relationship, but if we weren't looking for it, we wouldn't be in the game in the first place, now would we? But, I guess you knew all of this already. Well, I'm glad you did because I didn't. Let me tell you how I found out.

Who am I? You'll find out in due time. For now, all you need to know is that I'm a concerned friend of the two people who are about to tell you their stories. So just sit back and relax. Like my granny says when we go to the grocery store, "This gon' take awhile, baby!"

Part I
The Beginning: Training Day

Chapter 1
Jaslyn

Fort Worth, Texas 1980

Never in a million years had I dreamt of seeing a man so beautiful. He was my sister's friend. His name was Lloyd, and he was fine. He was at least six feet tall, and he had smooth, caramel skin. His hazel eyes were shaped like almonds and they complimented his black wavy afro. From the minute I saw him, I fell in love. Completely. Unequivocally. There was no doubt. We would be married, and he would take care of me. There was one problem. He was seventeen, and I was seven!!

But if he could just hold on until I was eighteen, he would see that I was the perfect woman for him. I was cute and smart. My honor roll certificates proved it, and I would be the perfect wife for him. I knew it. He would know it too as soon as he realized that I wasn't just a kid but a mature young lady who had so much love to give. There was no way he wouldn't want to be with me.

I know this sounds like the crazy ravings of a lovesick child, and they probably are; yet, this was me, Jaslyn Davenport, at seven years old. Lloyd is the first memory I have of being in love or having a crush, and I truly thought I could have a relationship with him.

My oldest sister, Carol, was extremely popular. She and my other two sisters, Francine and Melissa, were friends with all of the football and basketball players from their high school. Carol had actually been chosen as the football sweetheart the year she graduated. They weren't whores, mind you (I have to clarify this statement because some people associate football sweethearts with sluts). But, they were down to earth, and my mother wouldn't let any child go hungry; therefore, people tended to gravitate to our home. Every weekend, our house was filled with throngs of muscular young men looking to hang out, relax, and get a loving, home-cooked meal. Since my sisters were several years older than me, I was always surrounded by boys who were at least twice my age, and Lloyd was one of them.

Lloyd played forward for the basketball team, so he had a physique that was lean and powerful. Though he was tall, he was not intimidating. His friendly nature made him seem almost apologetic for being attractive. Lloyd was good-looking, but so were all the other players who came to the house. The reason I had goo-goo eyes over Lloyd was because he paid attention; he actually talked to me. He didn't just treat me like Carol's chubby baby sister who constantly got in the way. I wasn't a nuisance. He talked to me and listened to what I had to say as if I were his age. To a kid of seven who was used to being around adults that treated her like a child, being treated like an adult among adults was heaven on earth.

Lloyd talked to me about school. He told me that it was important for young girls to work hard and keep their heads in the books. From then on, I worked extra hard to stay on the honor roll. I even made the "A" honor roll once. Lloyd also talked to me about sports, especially his favorite—basketball (of course). He explained that the best team on the entire planet was the L.A. Lakers. Every Sunday after that, I was glued to the television with my mother, who was an avid sports fan, inhaling all the basketball I could. And guess who became my favorite team? You got it. The Lakers. What serious sports fan didn't like Kareem and Magic?

One Friday night, Lloyd, Carol, Francine and their friend, Gary, were discussing some friends of theirs who were dating. In the midst of a heated argument about infidelity, Carol blurts out "Well, if she had waited on 'Mr. Right,' she wouldn't be having these problems!" Curious, I asked, "Who is Mr. Wright?" Lloyd proceeded to explain.

"Jaslyn," he said, "'Mr. Right' is every girl's fantasy. In a woman's mind, he's the perfect man. Every woman has an ideal man who she believes will love her forever and unconditionally. You see, everyone has someone they're made for. Someone they're meant to spend the rest their lives with. For women, 'Mr. Right' is this person. He's the perfect match. He's intelligent, and handsome, and when these two people meet, they fall instantly in love. Some women feel that 'Mr. Right' is the man that God has planned for them since creation–their soul mate."

Lloyd again forgot he was talking to a seven–year–old child, and he forgot to mention the part that this theory was simply that–a theory. I didn't know that what he said lacked credibility, that "Mr. Right" was a figment of many women's very active imaginations.

I was glued to every word. In fact, I blurted without thinking, "Like you!"

"What?" Lloyd asked.

I explained with my chest puffed out, clearly proud that I found "Mr. Right" so early, "Like you! And me! When we get married." Carol, Francine, and Melissa shouted simultaneously, "GIRL, SHUT UP!"

Lloyd, always the consummate gentleman, told them to leave me alone. "Man, she don't know. Y'all leave her alone. Look, Jazz, you're a sweet kid, but you have to remember that I'm too old for you. You're a cute girl, and one day you will find someone who will fall deeply in love with you, but 'Mr. Right' is probably going to be someone closer to your age. Now maybe if you were older…but at your age…we just couldn't. I don't want to hurt your feelings or anything. You understand? Don't you Jazz?"

"Yes," I said softly, but I was deeply crushed. My sister Carol could see the hurt on my face. I was never one to mask my emotions. Every feeling…every thought I've ever owned could always be seen by the transparent expressions displayed on my face, no matter how hard I tried to hide it, and that day was no different. Quickly, Carol called to our mother, "Mama, come get Jaslyn."

I was whisked away, just like that, before the first tear could fall, and it surely did–in the kitchen with my mother. However, that day, I vowed to find "Mr. Right," the man who would love me completely. Perfectly. I locked that thought away in my heart. Tight and deep. I also vowed that no one would ever have the chance to hurt me the way Lloyd had.

Women learn two things about men. First, we learn the "Mr. Right" theory, usually taught to us by men. The lesson may not be as direct as the one from Lloyd. It is sometimes learned through the actions of a father figure or through lessons from the preachers at our churches or older brothers who protect and care for us, but invariably, women learn to wait on the perfect man.

Our next lesson, however, usually comes from a woman. If men could learn how women think in terms of who they are, it would probably save them a lot of trouble in trying to figure us out–you know, sit in our brains for a minute, eavesdrop on a waiting–to–exhale session–they would understand why we give them such a hard time. My first lesson about the role men play in a woman' s life came just after Lloyd proceeded to crush my fragile ego. The next lesson came the very same day. It came from my mother. Virginia Davenport gave me her own brand of advice. Having overheard the conversation, my mother set out to destroy all that Lloyd had taught me.

"Baby girl," she said, "You don't need a man to take care of you. Always understand that you can't trust men. You can't rely on them. Trusting a man always leads to heartache and pain because all men are dogs."

"What you mean? They all bark?

"No! Didn't you learn about metaphors in school? What I mean is that men are no good. They are no good to women because they eventually end up mistreating them in some way. Male dogs are never faithful. They mate with whatever female that's available, and men behave the same way. Whatever woman close enough for 'em to breathe on is who they will sleep with, and it doesn't matter if they already have a woman because they can never stay with the same one. It's their nature. Part of who they are. That's why you can never depend on a man. Not for anything. Take care of yourself. That way you don't have to worry about getting your heart broke, and you'll always know where your next meal is coming from."

So right there in the kitchen, sitting at a table among a ton of dishes, an empty pot of spaghetti, amid a haze of cigarette smoke so thick I could have easily been at a bingo hall, my house became a sort of classroom. A school where you receive lessons that no college professor could ever teach. First lesson—it's a man's job to take care of you. Second—never trust a man to do it.

My mother was right. I had put my feelings out there for Lloyd, laid them all on the table, and he crushed them. Trampled on them like Godzilla did Tokyo, and he did it in front of everyone without even considering how it would even affect me. He broke my heart.

I tried to erase Lloyd's earlier lesson from my mental thoughts, but it was too late. Underneath my mother's attempt to shield me from heartache was a vision of hope. If given the right opportunity, a vision of love, thoughts that "Mr. Right" actually existed. The error was not in the theory but in my plan to find him. I deduced that my mistake was going after Lloyd. Not letting him come to me. If I had waited until he was ready for me, ready to see me for who I really was, then there would have been no rejection because, in essence, he would have chosen me. Consequently, I chose to wait until "Mr. Right" found me. The plan was foolproof. By waiting on "Mr. Right" to choose me, I would protect my heart, but I would be prepared when he decided to reveal himself.

Yet, even fortified with the knowledge of a man's power to control a woman's emotions, I never forgot what Lloyd said about "Mr. Right," and somehow, the two lessons became fused into some type of twisted quest—the desire to find a man that was perfect for me, all the while believing that I never would. This, I suspect, is the dilemma that most women face. We receive dichotomous pieces of information. Unable to deal with them, we forge them together, and then, spend most of our lives looking for a person who doesn't exist. He doesn't exist because we can't allow him to. It's impossible. We are looking for the perfect person for us. Someone who loves us and cares for us. But even the slightest imperfection is cause for dismissal. Sensing the beginning of future heartache, we begin to think, "Oh no! Here it comes. Here it comes. Here comes the Dog. I knew I couldn't trust him." What man could hold up under such disastrous conditions? They don't.

Men don't know we think like this. Hell, we don't even know we think like this; thus, the problem. How can we fix what we don't know is there? These lessons are buried in our subconscious and reinforced with every relationship we ever have. Every unsuccessful relationship (including those that end because they are not right for us) is a constant reminder that we can never trust a man. If our dad, uncle, or brother fails us in some way (didn't get that car, wouldn't buy those shoes, didn't pay the bills), their failure only adds further evidence to the Black woman's credo, "Never trust a man!" If the men who already love us let us down, you can just imagine the heartache caused by a lover. We wear a protective shield over our hearts and while looking for someone to remove the shield, we are secretly waiting for him to remove it and *break it*. This is our pattern. It is self-destructive. It is misguided. But over and over we miseducate ourselves in love in order to receive love. This is our quest…at least it was mine.

Chapter 2
Freaky Sneaky

Jaslyn: October 1988

My quest begins with Kyle. His skin was the color of dark chocolate. He had two dimples that were so deep they looked liked valleys. His smile was infectious. When he turned those dimples on you, you couldn't help but feel good about yourself. You know…he was just cute, and most importantly, he fit the criteria–he liked me first.

He spoke to me every day. "Hey, Jaslyn. When you gon' let me call you?" He knew I liked it too because when I smiled he kept at it. "Come on, girl. Let me call you. You know I like you." I did like Kyle, but I was not about to let him know that.

We lived in a community that consisted of old black families. Teachers, preachers, domestics, janitors, and doctors were linked by a desire to own a home and the will to make a better life for their children. The streets of the Southside of Fort Worth were lined with sycamore trees, pecan trees, and brick–style bungalows. The neighborhood was quiet and usually serene even though it had a reputation for being a din for pimps, crackheads, and gangsters. During the eighties and following the inevitable consequences that Reaganomics had on many black families, we had more than our share of the criminal elements walking the streets, but everyone knew each other and treated each other like family. So, watching J.T. "the Crack Head" walking the streets trying to sell toothpaste or pork chops to make a buck was not unusual. You simply exchanged pleasantries about your families and went about your business.

"Hey J.T.! How you doin'?"

"Oh, hey Jazz, how you doin'?" He'd smile and scratch an unseen itch.

"Fine."

"How's your mama? She still making them tea cakes?" To black people in the South, teacakes were a delicacy–a pastry of superior quality on par with the scones of England. Well, maybe not that fancy, but you know what I mean.

"Not in a while."

"Aw, man. That's too bad. Her teacakes are the shit! I sure wouldn't mind havin' one right about now. Tell her I said hello."

"I sure will."

This was the basic conversation with any person in our neighborhood, whether it was between a girl and a crack head or a doctor and a pimp. Everyone was familiar with each other. Hell, J.T. was probably walking down the street to smoke with your cousin or to meet your daddy for a drink, so how could you judge him or look down on him? You couldn't. All anyone could do was to try and protect their families from the dangers of the neighborhood by raising them under strict rules and guidelines. I was raised under the watchful eye of a mother who held you at arms reach. You didn't go anywhere without Mama Davenport's permission and without her knowing exactly whom you were with or where and when you were with them. Under such restraints, it was hard to date anyone, especially Kyle Thompson, who had a reputation for doing things with girls my mother knew I wasn't ready for…but I still liked him.

Kyle and I were both exposed to this familial environment, but boys were given a bit more room in which to move when it came to dating. Consequently, while my mother was trying to protect me from him, his father was probably trying to give him pointers on how to get at me.

All of our lives, we were around each other. I knew who he was, and he knew who I was; however, we rarely talked or associated with the same circle of friends. Kyle did not start talking to me until I was fifteen, and he was seventeen. He was cordial up until this point, but the summer before my sophomore year, something changed in our relationship. I don't know what it was. Maybe, it was the fact that I spent the whole summer riding my bike and the baby fat I was sportin' when I was seven was no longer an issue. I rode for fun, but an added benefit of riding through the hood was that I shed twenty lbs., and I was getting attention from guys for my newly acquired womanly figure. With a small waist and well-rounded hips, my fifteen year-old frame could pass for twenty-five. My small breasts and baby face were the only thing that saved me from lecherous, old men. After a brief battle with acne in middle school, my dark skin was smooth and almost entirely free from blemishes and pimples. Whatever the reason, Kyle decided he wanted to get to know me better.

True to my word, I tried to make him work for my attention. School started in September. Although Kyle and I went to separate schools, our bus stops were across the street from each other. Evans Avenue was the main thoroughfare, which ran north and south through our neighborhood, and Mulkey Street intersected Evans from the east and west. I caught the bus on the east side of Evans and Mulkey, and Kyle caught the bus on the west side. Every day, he would call across the street amidst a mob of parents going to drop off their kids at Morningside Elementary School a block away from our bus stops.

"Hey, Jaslyn! How you doin', girl?" And then he would smile. His dimples twinkling in the morning sun.

"Fine," I would say flatly trying my best to hide an inward smile.

Every day the routine was the same until the beginning of October. Kyle resolved to intensify his game. There was a convenience store on the corner of the street where I lived. My house was two doors down so visitors to the store could see my family as we sat on the steps of the front porch. One day, Kyle spotted me and stopped by. He always started with the same greeting, "Hey, Jazz! What you doin', girl?"

"Nothing."

"I saw you sittin' here, and I decided to stop by."

"Oh." Flirting was not one of my many talents and skills.

"When you gon' let me call you?"

"Huh?"

"Call you? Girl, you know I like you. Stop trippin'!" he said smiling.

"Boy, you're crazy."

"I know I'm crazy. I'm crazy about you," he said as he sat next to me on my front step. That's when it happened. Everything changed in me. It was a combination of his scent and his nearness. He wore Obsession, a popular Calvin Klein cologne at the time. It accomplished its task because I was obsessed. Intoxicated by his aroma, Kyle had my full attention. I tried to maintain control while we chatted a little more, but before he left, Kyle had my number.

He called. We talked. What we said really doesn't matter. All that matters is that we talked everyday for the next two weeks. We talked on the phone and he came over everyday. Kyle gave me my first kiss; I'll never forget him.

It was the middle of October when Kyle and I started dating, so it would be dusk by the time he made it to my house after school. One night when he came over, my best friend Lisa Simmons was over visiting. We were complete opposites. She had fair skin and jet-black, curly hair, which made her seem Hispanic. She was tall and slender, and had it not been for her having almost a full "C" cup by the time she was in the seventh grade, Lisa could have been mistaken for an extremely feminine boy. She lived across the street with her mother, and we had been friends, literally, all of our lives so she knew all of my secrets, especially those involving Kyle.

Lisa and I were sitting on the front porch laughing about how our neighbor and friend, Nico, had gotten a beating for throwing mud at Mr. Kitchen. His mother did not waste any time issuing the beat down—she beat his butt right in front of the whole neighborhood. We respected Nico enough not to embarrass him by laughing in his face, but when he went in the house, we laughed so hard we cried. We were still laughing when Kyle walked up.

"What's so funny?"

"You, fat head!" Lisa challenged. For some reason, she did not like Kyle, but she could never say why. Whenever I asked her about it she always said it was just something about him that made her feel uncomfortable, and she thought I was too good for him.

"Why you trippin', Lisa? I haven't done anything to you."

"Who says I'm trippin'? Anyway, why are you always over here bothering Jaslyn? She's only pretending to like you so she won't hurt your feelings!" We all knew this was a lie.

Kyle simply smirked and said, "Is that right, Jazz? Are you just pretending?"

Lisa jumped in before I could respond, "Hell yeah, I'm right! You just gettin' on her nerves. Don't nobody like your black ass!"

"Jazz," Kyle questioned me again, "Is that right?"

I took the coward's way out. I feigned innocence in order to protect my feelings, and so I wouldn't look sprung because I just couldn't lie. "I'm not in that conversation. That's between you and Lisa. Keep me out of it."

Kyle sat down next to me. "Come on Jazz, tell the truth. Do you like me?" I looked away, afraid to look him in the eyes because the truth was evident on my face.

"I'm not in that. Lisa started this mess, not me," I said quietly.

"You're right; she did start it but you finish it. Tell me how you feel."

"You know how I feel. I talk to you everyday."

"Yes, you do but you never tell me how you feel. I need to know if I'm wasting my time. Tell me how you feel, Jazz." My head was still turned in the opposite direction. Kyle reached around and touched my chin with his hand and gently turned my head toward him. His voice was low and rhythmic. He said, "Better yet, show me how you feel." He leaned in, and his lips touched mine. They were soft and moist. It was like drinking a cold glass of water on a hot summer's day— refreshing. His tongue searched for mine and massaged it. I tried to pull away, but he found my tongue again and again as if he couldn't get enough. I was dizzy with desire. His arms enveloped me, and I felt at home. Safe and secure. I knew I'd found my place—in the arms of Kyle Thompson.

He eventually released me. He looked me in my eyes, "You do like me, don't you Jazz?"

"Yes." I said, my voice barely a whisper. Kyle smiled and I fell in love.

"You punked out!" I forgot that Lisa was still with us. I should have been embarrassed, but I wasn't. Kyle had me from that moment on, and he knew it.

Kissing led to making out each night on the front porch of my house. With the porch light out, the only light provided by the moon and the occasional headlights of a passing car, Kyle would kiss my neck, and his hand would reach under my shirt and caress my breasts. As he continued to kiss me, his hand would raise my bra and eventually his mouth would find my nipples. His moist lips felt like fire against my skin. As he fed on my breasts, his hand would unzip my pants. Kyle's fingers parted my other lips and explored my inner most parts until my body trembled with ecstasy.

As I moaned with the pains of desire, my mind was experiencing another kind of pain. Guilt. Not just the guilt of getting freaky on my mama's front porch, but the guilt of doing something that I knew was a sin. Years of training in the Young Women's Auxiliary at church regarding the perils and pitfalls of fornication surfaced at a time when I felt I was experiencing one of the greatest joys of my life. My mind was saying, "Wait. Stop. No. Don't. No, no," but my mouth was saying, "Yes. Yes. Don't stop. Don't stop!" And Kyle didn't. He used his fingers to show me pleasure that at 15 years old, I never would have imagined.

"Oh God," I thought, "Why am I doing this? This is wrong. This is so wrong."

All these thoughts ran through my mind and just as Kyle would begin to take me to that next level, outside on my mother's porch—I would stop him. I would push him away and say, "It's time for you to go home. I don't want to get in trouble." Looking back, I remember that he never became angry. He would always fix my clothes, kiss me goodnight, and call me when he got home to see if I actually got in trouble.

Kyle taught me that love could be tender. I always felt that Kyle loved me because he cared enough to check on me. I never would have thought that it was a ruse.

This erotic cat–and–mouse game went on for several weeks. Soon, Kyle started inviting me over to his house. I was naïve, but I was not by any means stupid. I knew what that invitation included, and to some degree, I wanted to accept. However, I took my time figuring out if I wanted to go all the way with Kyle. In the back of my mind, I still believed in "Mr. Right" and that I should save myself for him, but I was hesitant about sleeping with Kyle because I think I knew he wasn't "the one."

I guess Kyle got tired of me getting mine, and he wasn't getting his. He called one day and said he had something to tell me.

"What is it?"

"I'm getting back with my ex-girlfriend."

"Huh?"

"I'm getting back with my ex-girlfriend."

"What ex-girlfriend?" Throughout the few weeks we had been dating, Kyle and I had never discussed our previous relationships. I didn't have any, so it was not at the forefront of my mind. Huge mistake.

"Her name is Tamara, and I have a baby by her."

"What the hell? Baby? What baby? When did this shit happen? How old is the baby? Why the fuck am I just now hearing about it?" The questions rolled off my lips like a barrage of bullets in a drive-by shooting.

"The baby is six months old, and I broke up with Tamara two months after the baby was born. I wanted to tell you, but I was afraid that you would have never given me a chance."

"You've got that shit right."

"I know you're mad, and I don't want to hurt you. I want to be there for my daughter. I'm not in love with Tamara like I am with you. I just need to be there for my child. I want to be a better man than my father." Kyle's confessions made me love him even more. His father was a philanderer and an abuser. He was dating one of our neighbors who stayed around the corner from Kyle's house. Kyle always talked to me about how he hated the fact that his father disrespected his mother so easily. I believed he was trying to do the right thing for his daughter, and I knew I was not mature enough to be in a relationship with a boy who had a baby.

I was thinking. The phone was silent. "You understand? Don't you, Jazz?" Those two questions again. Would all the men in my life want me to understand when they broke my heart? No, I didn't understand. Why the fuck did he pick me? He knew he had issues when he met me. He came after me. He could have left me alone, and I would not be hurting right now. I felt like he had my lungs in his hands and was squeezing them until I couldn't breathe. Pride will leave you broke and hungry, but it will also protect you when you need to maintain your dignity. Hell no, I didn't understand; I didn't ask for that shit, but I would never let him know how badly he'd hurt me.

"Yeah, I understand."

I moped around for three days trying to figure out what the hell went wrong. How did I allow the man I loved to slip away? Maybe there was still hope for us. That hope was crushed when I went to school the next day.

At breakfast that morning, I was telling one of my closest friends, Loretta Goodwin, about the break-up; what I didn't know was that she would add missing pieces to the enigma called Kyle.

"Get back with her," Loretta said incredulously, "Girl, they never broke up!"

"What?"

"Not only was he going with you and her, he was also going out with Ebony and Shantè, too."

"You mean Ebony Johnson in the eleventh grade and Shantè Richmond from church?"

"You mean you didn't know? I thought you knew. Everybody knows that Kyle is a dog. That's why I never said anything. I thought you knew, too!"

"No, I didn't know that. I knew he had sex, but I didn't know he was having sex with every damn body! How was I supposed to know that?"

"Everybody on the south side knows about Kyle. You remember the day he took you home from school? Well, he was really here to pick up Ebony, but you saw him first and got in the car. That's why I thought you knew. I thought you were trying to pour salt in his game."

"No, I thought he was just hanging out. I bummed a ride home so I wouldn't have to ride the bus for a change."

"Are you okay? Do you need to talk? What are you going to do to him?" I looked at Loretta and burst out laughing. I laughed hysterically for about five minutes.

"Girl, why are you laughing? This shit ain't funny!"

"Oh, yes it is. It is funny, and I should have known better." I should have known better. I should have listened to my mother.

Chapter 3
Sampson

Fort Worth, Texas

I don't know why women are so crazy, but I do know one thing. I'm tired of fooling with them. Sick to death. There's just one problem—I love them too much to leave them alone! I'm just sick of getting my feelings hurt. No matter what I do, I always seem to come out on the bottom, and I refuse to do it anymore.

Forgive me, I didn't mean to drone on. Let me introduce myself. My name is Sampson Tate, and I've tried hard to honor women and respect them. It just doesn't seem to work. As a boyfriend, I do my best to make a woman feel wanted. I let her know that I appreciate her and her time. Sending flowers just to say I'm thinking about you. Calling out of the blue. Cooking dinner and giving foot massages. While going through all of these experiences, I've learned something. As soon as you give a woman the slightest bit of affection, she starts to trip. I mean they seriously start to act a damn fool. It's like Dr. Jekyll and Ms. Hyde, or should I say Dr. Jekyll and Ms. Drama. Because that's exactly who they become—DRAMA Queens! Paging you all day. Acting an ass because you want to hang out with the fellas. Checking your voice mail. Even riding by the apartment to see if you are actually at home. Sidebar: I caught one girl I was dating, LaRhonda, doing a drive-by one day after I told her I was staying in for the evening, and I didn't want to come over to her place. She was pissed. Started accusing me of cheating and then slammed the phone down in my face. I figured she was checking up on me because when I looked out of the window, I saw her pass by my apartment in her car several times, but she never came upstairs.

It seems as if some women equate affection with enslavement. You go out with them for a good two weeks, and they try to get you to pay their rent, their light bill, their car payment, and buy their groceries. Soon, I'm working just to pay their bills. I have to get a part time job to meet my expenses, and I have my own business! One girl even asked me to give her $500.00 so she could send her dog to obedience school. *Now ain't that a bitch?*

Women feel that relationships are a prime opportunity to take advantage of a brother. In a sense, you have to submit to them. Tell them all your secrets. You have to let them in your life and prove to them how much you love them. If you're not spending every waking hour with them, you don't care. You start going to events you don't want to be at to make them feel secure. It's sickening. Pretty soon your boys are calling you whipped and ripping you up because you can't seem to do one single thing without her.

Women have a solution for the pussy-whipped theory, too: they start telling you that your homeboys are trash. They begin to pinpoint every character flaw of every friend you've ever known or hung-out with. "Why do you hang with Jawaan? He's so immature. All he wants to do is play basketball and X-Box all day." "Malik is such a dog. Why must you go out with him all of the time? Are you doing the same things he's doing? You know birds of a feather flock together?" Basically, they try to persuade you into thinking that nothing is wrong with the relationship; something must be wrong with your friends for not understanding that when two people are in love they should be together – ALL THE FUCKIN' TIME. Pretty soon, you stop kicking it with the fellas just so you won't have to listen to her nagging ass. After they've drained you of every ounce of masculinity and self-respect you have, all you're left with is an empty bank account and a limp dick. And, that's when your friends light you up for being whipped.

I'm sick of it. Instead of trying to play Lothario to the lonely, I should have listened to my uncle when he said to never trust a woman. I thought he was crazy because of the way he treated my aunt, and she was my heart. She took my younger brother, Solomon, and me in and raised us when my mom was strung out on drugs. Because of her kindness and generosity, I was resigned to never treat a woman the way my Uncle Junior treated my Aunt Tootie.

Aunt Tootie was beautiful. She had long silky hair, and skin the color of honey. If her hair and skin didn't make you take notice, then her perfect hourglass figure definitely would. Her real name was Camille, but no one called her that but Uncle Junior. He always said it with such venom that somewhere between his tongue and your ear, the name lost its beauty.

"Camille! Get yo' black ass in here and wash them damn dishes!" Uncle Junior always had a habit of mumbling to himself once he issued his commands and orders.

"That bitch think I'm crazy. She know that kitchen dirty. I don't play that," he would say to himself. Then, to reinforce his authority, "Next time, I'm gon' knock yo' ass out!" He would too. He hit Aunt Tootie so much that eventually her glowing honey-colored complexion grew dull and dark from the bruises she endured from his fists. Her skin no longer felt smooth and soft but was leathery and bumpy to touch, which always made me sad because I used to love the feel of her skin next to mine when she gave me a hug.

Not only did he beat her but he cheated on her, as well. She couldn't have any kids, so he used that as an excuse to sleep around. It is rumored that out of wedlock Junior Wilson fathered so many kids that he had enough to start his very own Head Start Day Care Center. Aunt Tootie knew about Junior's affairs, but I believe she put up with his behavior because she felt guilty that she was unable to conceive.

Every day, Junior broke Camille's heart. He slept around and broke her heart. He beat her and broke her heart. He lost his job and broke her heart. He got shot and broke her heart. Reverend Jenkins, who discovered that Junior had gotten his wife pregnant, shot Junior in the ass at a pool hall when I was sixteen. He developed gangrene in his right butt cheek and had to have his leg amputated when the infection spread. Aunt Tootie spent the rest of her life taking care of him because he could never work again.

I knew I could never break a woman's heart the way Junior broke Tootie's. I also vowed to keep a job, stay faithful, and never put my hand on a woman no matter how bad she made me feel, but every day, it's becoming harder to keep that vow.

Chapter 4
Concentration

Sampson: Stop Six, Texas 1984

Every relationship I've ever had has tested my commitment to treating a woman with respect. I've finally realized that there isn't a woman on earth worthy of my time. I mean let's face it–I'm a sensitive, caring, handsome, black man with an education and a very healthy financial package. I'm an inch shy of six feet tall; my hair is naturally curly, and it's cut close and neat. But, I leave just enough hair on top for a woman to run her fingers through it. My skin tone is a smooth, honey-brown, a perfect complement to my immaculately manicured goatee and mustache. Most women compliment me on my brown eyes, muscular build from years of playing sports, and my bowlegs. The "Denzel" swagger doesn't hurt, either. Not to brag or anything, but I do have my shit together, and women need to appreciate that shit.

My love life has been one disappointment after another. The only woman who has never disappointed me was my first love, Mrs. Mayfield. She was my fifth grade teacher at Dunbar Elementary School. I don't know how old she was, but she was beautiful. I loved Mrs. Mayfield. Her voice was soft and melodic, and she made school interesting. It was like she was hypnotizing me into learning. Until this day, I still measure women according to her standards. Is she tall? Is her skin smooth and soft? Is her hair long and silky? Can she entice me with her conversation? Mrs. Mayfield was all those things for me, and from her, I learned this: being poor and black is no excuse for being ignorant, lazy, and unmotivated. No matter what color we were, she wanted us to strive for greater things, to learn more about the world, to rise above our circumstances, and to show people that we were a force to be reckoned with. For extra credit, she had our class put up campaign signs for various elections and to assist with voter registration drives. As a class we read not just about Martin Luther King, Jr. but also about Malcolm X, Marcus Garvey, and Mary McLeod Bethune.

She wanted us to see that color did not determine our success but our ability to persevere and endure did. I learned a lot from Mrs. Mayfield. I especially learned that being stupid is not a requirement to being sexy. Intelligence is DAMN SEXY!!

She could discuss any topic with ease and fervor. If an issue was new to her, she always seemed to ask enough probing questions until she became familiar with it. Every time she stood in front of the class my, heart would stop because I knew she was about to speak. I knew what Mrs. Mayfield had to say came with great thought and care, and so I anticipated each lesson. I still love Mrs. Mayfield. I always will.

Alicia Matthews had a hard time filling in Mrs. Mayfield's shoes as the love of my life, but she was my first girlfriend. She fit the checklist to a tee. She was tall, 5'5" to be exact, which, in the eighth grade was gargantuan, especially for a girl. She was pretty. I still remember the feel of her skin. It was as soft as silk. Her light brown hair cascaded down her back in a long braided ponytail and landed in the middle of her shoulder blades. Yet, Alicia's greatest asset was her brain. She was an "A" honor roll student in a magnet school, already taking ninth grade courses. When she transferred to my school from Dallas, I was smitten. No girl at Dunbar Middle School could light a candle to her, and I wanted her to be my girl.

I saw an opportunity to get to know her when I realized that we had a mutual interest in chess. At chess club practice one afternoon, I was concentrating on moving my knight to capture Orandis Jones' queen. This would be the move to solidify my position as Dunbar's greatest chess player. His king would be in check, and the game would be virtually over. If I made this move, it didn't matter where he placed his king to save him; he would always be in jeopardy of capture. The game could also go the other way if I made a mistake, so I had to be careful. I wanted to beat Orandis more than I wanted my little brother, Solomon, to stop wetting the bed and pushing me over in the wet spot.

Orandis was a grade "A" asshole. He was from one of the wealthiest black families in Fort Worth. The only reason he went to Dunbar was because he was in the magnet program for smart kids; otherwise, he would have been at Country Day or the Oakridge School, private schools attended by mostly rich white kids. But, Old Man Jones loved to save a buck, so he sent Orandis to Dunbar so that he could receive, as he put it, a "superior education for free." Orandis never let you forget that you were his economic and intellectual inferior. In some small way, he always reminded you that you were privileged to be in his presence. I wanted to beat his ass at chess to show him that a broke black brother from the hood could whip him mentally and introduce him to reality.

I was concentrating, trying to anticipate Orandis' counter-move, making sure he would have nowhere else to turn, but then, Alicia walked in the room. At that moment, all rational thought escaped from my mind. We had absolutely no girls in chess club, yet the prettiest girl in the whole school had just walked in the door. I was dumbfounded. In my anxiety, I moved a pawn and freed up my king. Checkmate. Orandis had me. He boasted so loudly that I am sure my face turned beet red.

"Sampson! How could you make such a stupid mistake? I thought for sure you had me cornered. You obviously are not the opponent I thought you to be. I'll think twice before I choose you as my practice partner again. I'll never improve my game by playing with someone who makes such ghastly mistakes. Really, you neighborhood kids could really benefit from some of the logic classes offered by the magnet program. It would improve your thinking abilities."

"I am in magnet, Orandis."

"Well, maybe you should be in regular classes then because there is no way I should have beaten you."

The entire chess club had stopped in their tracks. All ten of them, including Alicia Matthews, who was suppressing a giggle. I was mortified. I did manage to grunt at Orandis, "Kiss my ass, punk!" I wanted to slap the shit out of Orandis, but I refused to embarrass myself any further. I left practice with a bruised ego, certain that I had lost all my chances with the girl of my dreams.

As I left school, my best friends, Malik Wallace and Jawaan Turner, caught up to me. They were just leaving football practice, and they reeked of sweat and grass—a very lethal combination but I was accustomed to the smell. We walked to and from school together, everyday. Stop Six could be a treacherous neighborhood, and people tended to hang in groups in order to feel secure.

If ever there was a city within a city, Stop Six, Texas was it. Located on the southeast edge of Fort Worth, the neighborhood was a living and breathing landmark. Formally known as Cowanville, Stop Six gained its name because it was the sixth stop on an old train line that ran between Dallas and Fort Worth. The residents would proudly tell you that they lived in an historic African-American locale. We had our own heritage and identity apart from the city. We were known for our barbershops and barbeque joints—we call them joints and not restaurants because most of the time you were standing outside ordering your food through a window with bars on it. We were also the home of the state champion Dunbar High School Wildcats basketball team and Coach Robert Hughes. Almost every year, generations of Fort Worth families traveled to Austin to see Coach Hughes and the Wildcats play in the championship tournament. We had a lot to be proud of, but we also had a lot of things for which we were infamous. Gang banging and dope dealing were two of them. If you fell in with the wrong crowd, you could quickly become victims of both. But, the people in Stop Six were also loyal; therefore, when you found friends that you could trust, you stuck with them. So when I met Jawaan and Malik in the fifth grade, I knew that we would be friends for life.

Jawaan stayed across the street, and Malik lived on the same street two blocks down. I gravitated toward Malik and Jawaan because they were serious about their schoolwork and wanted to avoid the pitfalls of living in our neighborhood. We also shared a love of sports and break-dancing. They played football and basketball, and I played baseball. Break-dancing speaks for itself.

I quickly walked up Stalcup toward my house on Truman Avenue.

"Sam, hold up! What's up with you man? Why you walking so fast today?" Jawaan asked when he caught up to me.

Malik chimed in, "Yeah, man, you tryin' to leave us or something?"

"No, we got out of chess club early."

"Did you whip Orandis' ass? Please tell me you shut his punk ass up!"

"No. I lost," I said flatly.

"Stop playin' fool! You lost? For real?" Jawaan could not believe his ears. I had been talking about beating Orandis for weeks.

"You trippin'. I know you did not lose to Orandis Jones. You could beat his ass with one hand tied behind your back. You play way better than he does. What the fuck happened?" Malik was irate. He took this loss personally. His father used to work at one of the Jones' grocery stores, but he was fired two years earlier for showing up drunk on the job. Mr. Wallace showed up the next day to beg for his job back because he had a wife and five kids to feed, but Old Man Jones wasn't having that. He berated Mr. Wallace in front of his co-workers. He proceeded to say that Mr. Wallace was a drain on society's resources and a waste of human life because he was too stupid to hang on to a good-paying job and provide for his family. Jones drove the stake further into Mr. Wallace's heart by explaining, in a drawl so thick with pretension and contempt I'm sure Mr. Wallace felt like a sharecropper trying to make a living on Ol' Massa's farm, that he should be grateful to him for allowing him the opportunity to work for a black man of his stature for any length of time.

After that, Mr. Wallace began to drink more and more. He eventually went to the store one day to buy a 40 oz. bottle of beer, and he never came home. Mrs. Wallace was forced to get on welfare to support her family–in the Wallace family, a fate worse than death.

"Man, I had him beat, but I lost my concentration," I explained to Malik why I'd let him down.

"How?"

"I don't know. I just did, okay?" I was too ashamed to say that I had lost my concentration because the prettiest girl in school had walked in the room.

"Oh, you ain't gettin' off that easy. You mean to tell me that you've been gunning for Orandis all year and you finally get the chance, and you lose your concentration? Somethin's up. What the fuck happened?"

"Come on, give it up," Jawaan insisted.

Seeing no way out, I confessed. "Alicia Matthews walked in," I explained despondently.

They both looked at me with these dumbfounded expressions and said, "And?"

"She's pretty, alright! When I looked up at her, I lost my concentration and made a stupid mistake. I couldn't think straight."

"You mean you lost the biggest match of our lives because of some girl?!"

"*Our lives?* Who lost the match, Malik? Me or you?"

Jawaan interjected before Malik could respond. "You're crazy, fool!"

I sighed. "I know, but she's beautiful. I couldn't help myself."

"You're a sucker. You don't ever let a female make you lose your game. Get it?"

"Yeah, I get it." In his own way, Jawaan was saying to never allow a woman to make you lose your composure, but with our eighth grade vocabularies, and mentalities, this was as sophisticated as our conversation could get.

"So you like her, huh?" Jawaan was sympathetic, but Malik was still seething.

"Man, fuck that girl! She ain't all that."

"Man, watch your language. We gettin' close to the house." We had just recently learned how to curse, and we let the words flow freely away from our parents. We knew if they ever heard us, the beating we would receive would leave us bleeding for days. I continued, "I don't know what I'm going to do, but I like her."

"Don't worry about it, man. I'll help you out. J-Dog's on the case." Jawaan had a girlfriend for about a month by now, so he felt like a real ladies' man. And, he probably was, but I had my doubts.

Chapter 5
The Hook Up

Sampson: Two Weeks Later

Jawaan's idea of helping me out was passing a note. He wrote a letter to his friend, Tamika Clemmons, in 1ˢᵗ period English. Tamika was in love with Jawaan; even though he had a girlfriend, she was willing to do anything he asked in hopes of winning his affection and taking him from his girl. His reputation as a ladies man was strengthened by Jawaan's friendship with Tamika. His interest in the girl was limited to what he could get out of her: lunch money, homework, cassettes, and in this particular instance, information. Two weeks after my defeat to Orandis, I had what I needed to know.

He stopped me in the cafeteria during lunch to give me the low down.

"Man, guess what?"

"What?"

"I told you I was going to help you out, right?"

"Yeah. And?"

"Well, I did! Alicia thinks you're cute."

I was elated, but suspicion and curiosity consumed me. Tact and discretion were not characteristics that Jawaan was known for. No, in an effort to save time, he would most assuredly front you out in a way that only middle school students could.

"How do you know that?"

"She told Tamika."

"Why would she tell Tamika something like that?"

"Man, why all the questions? You should be happy."

"I just wanna know what happened. And I want to know how and why Tamika knows my business. You know that girl talks too damn much."

"Yeah, I know how she is, but look, here's what happened. I wrote a note to Tamika in 1ˢᵗ period. You know she likes me, right? She'll do whatever I tell her, so I asked her if she and Alicia were friends. She passed the note back, and it said that they were cool. Then she wanted to know why I wanted to know. 'Did I like her? Did I think she was cute' and all that? I was like, 'No'. I was asking for you. I wanted to know what Alicia thought about you. She wrote back and said that she would ask her during gym. After third period, I saw Mika in the hall, and she passed me another note. When I read it, she said that she asked Alicia during second period gym if she liked you. 'Mika told me that Alicia said she thought you were cute."

"Man, this is a bunch of he said-she said mess. How am I supposed to believe all that nonsense? You call this hooking a brother up?"

"It's called 'part of the plan'."

"Well, when do I get the rest of it?"

"Don't trip. You didn't have to be a chicken-shit. You could have asked the girl yourself, but, since I feel sorry for your scary behind, I'll still help you. Are you going to church tonight or what?"

"Yeah, tonight we have our Wednesday night bible study. I don't feel like going, but you know Aunt Tootie does not play when it comes to going to church. Shit!"

"What time do you get home?"

"About 8:30 or so. Why? What you got planned?"

"Just be home before nine o'clock, okay. I'm going to call you."

Weekday services at Amanda Street First Saints of the Apostle Missionary Baptist Church started at 7:00pm. Aunt Tootie, Solomon, and I got there at 6:45. Uncle Junior was on the corner of Stalcup and Berry drinking beer with his friends.

I went to bible study that night, but my mind definitely wasn't "stayed" on Jesus. As Brother Timms schooled the Youth Department on the perils of fornication and other vices, I was busy thinking about Alicia

She thought I was cute. All was right in my world. I just hated the fact that Brother Timms was teaching. He tended to get a little long-winded, and I wanted to be sitting by the phone at 8:30 on the dot.

My anxiety must have been evident on my face because Brother Timms caught me daydreaming and tried to call me out.

"Mr. Tate, what does the bible say about the dangers of the flesh?"

"Well, I think it says that the flesh is weak, but the spirit is strong...or something like that," I stammered.

"Well, Sampson, I see that you have been paying attention. Good job, son!" He patted me on the back and moved on to his next victim.

"Yes, sir. Thank you, sir," I said to his back. We didn't play that "yeah" and no" stuff when talking to adults. Even though I wanted to bust Brother Timms upside his head for fronting me out, I still had to show him the utmost respect. I was just glad I had been paying attention in Sunday school this week, or I would have been cold busted.

Luckily, bible study ended on time because Sister Timms wanted to get home and watch reruns of Perry Mason. I got home at 8:30, and I didn't have much time because Jawaan called me at 8:45 with Tamika on the phone.

"What's up, fool?" Jawaan gave the traditional ghetto greeting with a laugh. He knew I was sweating bullets, and he was enjoying every minute of it. I tried to play it cool, though.

"Nothing much. What's up with you?"

"Just looking out for you, that's all."

"Is that right?"

"Yeah. Tamika's on the phone. She's going to call Alicia for you."

"Naw, man! That's not even cool."

"Chill out, okay? She won't even know that you are on the phone. We got your back. Just Chill. You ready, 'Mika?"

"Yeah, hold on a minute."

As we waited in silence while Tamika dialed Alicia's number, I was a bundle of nerves. *What if this girl gets on the phone and says she really hates my guts and only said I was cute as a joke? Or what if she already had a boyfriend?* I felt powerless and vulnerable. I was petrified and anxious all at the same time. I would wonder no more. Alicia answered the phone.

"Hello, may I speak to Alicia?" Tamika tried to suppress a giggle that might expose her duplicitous deed.

"Speaking." One word and I was in a trance. I no longer cared about the fact that Tamika and Jawaan were on the phone. I just wanted to know if she liked me. That's all that mattered. *Did I have a chance?*

"This is Tamika."

"Hey, girl. What's up?"

"Nothing. What are you doing?"

"I'm studying for my Algebra test, but I can take a break. What's on your mind?"

"I was calling because I wanted to talk to you about something."

"What is it? Is it serious? What's wrong?"

"Oh, it's nothing like that. But it is serious to some people." Tamika, in her own sarcastic way, was trying to poke fun at my manhood, but I didn't care. I really wanted to curse her ass out right there, but I remained calm because I wanted to know if Alicia liked me more than I wanted to front Tamika out.

Alicia wasn't about to waste time with silly word games. She asked, "Well, what is it?"

Tamika, in her feeble interrogation, resumed her questioning from the day's previous activities.

"You know today in gym I asked you what you thought about Sampson Tate, right?"

"Yeah?"

"You said he was cute, right?" Tamika was trying to validate Jawaan's story. Alicia confirmed.

"Yes. So. Get to the point."

"You know I go with his best friend, Jawaan. He's on the phone, and he wants to know if Sampson can call you some time."

"Oh, does he now? I thought Jawaan was going with Carla Craig."

Feeling his back against the wall, Jawaan jumped in the conversation. Although he was down for helping me out, he didn't want it getting around the school that he was a two-timer. "Tamika, you know I don't go with you. You need to stop playing."

"Whatever, Jawaan! See if I buy you lunch again or do your homework!" Tamika was clearly pissed, but Jawaan managed to steer the conversation back in the right direction. "Anyway, who I'm dating is not the point. Can Sam call you or not?"

Alicia giggled softly, "Why is it so important that Sam call me? Does he like me or something?"

"Something like that."

Alicia was silent, and I waited. There was no turning back now. She knew the deal. I swear I heard the theme music from Jeopardy playing in the background.

Finally, a reprieve. "Sure, he can call me. Tamika, give him my phone number tomorrow at school. I have to finish studying for my test. I'll talk to you guys later."

In a huff, Tamika mumbled "Later" and a weak, "Bye, Jawaan." And both girls hung up their respective phones.

Jawaan whispered, "Let me make sure that my line is clear." He clicked twice and came back on the line. "It's clear. Now, you know that Tamika will never talk to me again, don't you."

"Yeah. Sorry about that."

"No problem. I'll miss the lunch money but not her worrisome ass. Anyway, you're my boy. I had to look out for you, but, after you get that number tomorrow everything is on you. I'm not in it. You got me?"

"Cool, man. I just needed to get my foot in the door. Thanks J."

"A'ight, fool. I'll holla' at you tomorrow. Peace."

"Peace."

Alicia and I talked on the phone everyday for a month. I even started walking her to class everyday, and everyone understood, especially my friends, that Alicia was my girlfriend.

Well, I guess it was understood by everyone– everyone that is, but Alicia.

Our eighth grade prom was a week away, and I was excited about making the preparations. I didn't want Alicia to worry about anything. In part because my pride didn't want her to know how poor I really was and also to prove I was a gentleman.

My Aunt Tootie worked overtime at Cowboys Cleaners to buy me a new suit and some new shoes. I knew I was a candidate for Prom King because I would be the best-dressed Negro at the prom in my navy blue, double-breasted suit and my navy blue alligator shoes.

I called Alicia to discuss plans for the dance.

"What color dress are you wearing?"

"Gold. Why?"

"Because I'm wearing blue."

"Oh."

"What time will you be ready?"

"I'll be dressed by six-thirty."

Before I could tell her what time I would be at her house, my Uncle Junior started tripping about me taking out the trash. I didn't want her to hear his drunk ass yelling at me, so I rushed off the phone. "Hey, my uncle wants me to take out the trash, so I'll talk to you tomorrow."

"Bye."

The night of the prom, I was so excited I was dressed by five o'clock. Alicia didn't live far from us so my Uncle Junior took me to pick her up at 6:15p.m. Ten minutes later, I was ringing Alicia's doorbell. Her twin answered. With her crows' feet and graying temple, Alicia's mother greeted me pleasantly at the door.

"Hello, Mrs. Matthews. It's nice to meet you. Is Alicia ready?"

"Yes, she is, but who are you?"

"I'm Sampson. Sampson Tate. Alicia's date for the prom." Perplexed didn't begin to describe how I was feeling. Mrs. Matthews had no idea who I was. Surely, Alicia would inform her mother about me since we had been dating for a month.

"Sampson, I am so sorry but there must be some type of misunderstanding because Alicia already has a date for the prom."

"Ma'am?"

As if on cue, Orandis Jones walked his chubby, pretentious ass up to the door with a corsage in his hand. His condescending smirk told me that I was not going to the prom with Alicia Matthews. Though I knew making my date happen was futile, I still had to try. I was not willing to suffer another defeat to Orandis without putting up a fight, especially since I had been engaged in this battle and didn't even know it. I had to talk to Alicia. There had to be an explanation. *Her mother was forcing her to go the prom with Orandis because he was rich. She probably knew who I was but didn't want her daughter to be associated with me because I was broke.* These thoughts raced through my mind as I tried to salvage my dignity and pride. It seems silly, but some black people in Fort Worth were obsessed with social status–however minimal it was.

If I can talk to Alicia, I might convince her that the fact that I'm poor won't harm our relationship. I'm a young man with ambition. I would eventually go places, I reasoned. All she had to do was convince her mother that I was a good guy born into circumstances I couldn't control. *If I could just talk to Alicia.* I found the courage to say, "Mrs. Matthews, may I speak to Alicia, please?"

"I don't know. I don't want no shit at my house." For a brief moment, Mrs. Matthews forgot about her education and reverted back to her soulful, East Texas beginnings. I refused to let her deter me from my task.

"Please, ma'am," I begged, "There won't be any trouble. I just want to find out what's going on."

She relented, "Alright, come on in." Mrs. Matthews went to the back of the house, and a few minutes later, the woman of the hour appeared, apparently oblivious to the problem at hand.

She was wearing a gold dress that stopped at her ankles. It was straight with spaghetti straps, and the satin material fell gently around her waist. Her long hair fell in deep waves on her shoulders, and it glistened with evidence of a recent trip to the salon. She was so beautiful that I almost forgot that she was about to stand me up. *Almost.* I fought the urge to reach for her hand. I was justifiably angry, and I wanted to know what the hell was going on so I asked, "What the hell happened?"

"*Excuse* me?"

I detected a bit of an attitude, but at this point, I didn't understand it or care about it. I wanted an answer. "What the *hell* is going on?"

"First of all, don't use language like that in my house. My mother can hear you."

"I'm sorry, but what's going on? Why is Orandis here? I thought I was your date for the prom!"

"Sampson, you never asked me to go to the prom with you."

"What? You're my girlfriend…you're supposed to go to the prom with me," I stammered.

"Who said I was your girlfriend?"

I was floored. I struggled to find words to define our relationship.

"Well…we…I thought…look, we talk on the phone everyday. I walk you to class everyday. You even let me kiss you the other day when I walked you home from school!"

"That doesn't mean that I'm your girlfriend. I have a lot of friends who happen to be boys, and I talk to them on the phone everyday. They are even willing to walk me to class or home from school if I let them. Just because I let you walk me to class, or home, does not mean that we're dating. It means that you want to spend time with me. That's cool, but you never said that you wanted to be my boyfriend.

"I let you kiss me because I like you, and I wanted to know if you could kiss, but that does not mean we go together. If you want to be my boyfriend, or take me to the prom, then you need to ask me. I only said yes to Orandis because you never asked."

I had nothing to say. I turned and walked out the door without uttering a single word. When I got in the car without Alicia my, Uncle Junior asked me what happened. All I could say was, "Let's go." In our old, dirty Buick with the rusty top, we headed home in total silence.

I felt love flicker like the beginning of a flame, and I had it snuffed out in an instant. Never one to stew, I was determined to move on, but now I had a new piece of information in my arsenal. Alicia gave me the power to see that relationships are not absolutes. Always say what you mean and never assume!

Part II
Heartbreak Hotel

Chapter 6
Where There's Smoke

Jaslyn: College, Freshman Year

My favorite song in the 1980s was "Heartbreak Hotel" by Michael Jackson. I don't think it was very popular, but it was one of his earlier cuts that helped establish his independence as a solo artist and build his reputation as a musical genius. This bittersweet song is a metaphor for the majority of my relationships. It succinctly describes the painful process of dating: building a house and tearing it down to establish new foundations because termites have eaten the old one. Cynical but true. I learned the hard way never to trust my instincts when it came to men. I have really bad judgment. After Kyle, I retreated into a world that was entirely my own. My self-confidence was shaken, and I didn't trust myself anymore. Other than riding my bicycle everyday, I spent the majority of my adolescence with my nose in a book or my eyes glued to the television. If I could have managed to watch T.V. and read a book at the same time, I would have been in heaven. I didn't want to date. I wanted to be safe, and men were definitely hazardous. After high school, I went to the University of Texas at Arlington to study social work with the plan to eventually go to law school and practice family law. Men would only derail my ambitions. No, I was not a student of Sappho, but I had to stay focused.

There were two men who managed to convince me that men were worthwhile, again. The first was Nathan, and the second was Lorenzo. I should have stopped with Nathan, but I didn't want to give up on love, so, even after all the shit, I went through with him, I still gave Lorenzo's busted ass a chance. Please, don't judge me. Remember my instincts were bad, and I had to learn from experience. I became hooked on an extremely bad cycle of falling in and out of love despite numerous signs that what I was doing wasn't working. I have always been the type to do things at full speed. I never do things halfway. I always give one hundred percent, so even when I fuck-up, I fuck-up royally. And, Nathan was a royal fuck-up (pun intended)!

After Kyle, I was emotionally traumatized. I tended to wear my heart on my sleeve when it came to men. I would always overanalyze situations while waiting for the right signal from them to make a move. As a result, I didn't have many boyfriends after Kyle for fear that I might get my feelings hurt. As Lisa might say, I was laying in the cut, and I needed to get my shit together and get back in the game.

I dated some but not often. I like to think that I was searching for quality and not quantity as so many of my friends did. I witnessed many of them run through men like cars at a racetrack, and they were still lonely and disappointed although they would never admit it. I concluded that if I could pick and choose whom I dated with discretion, and I still ended up like they did then, I was way ahead of the game.

Frankly, I knew Nathan was no good for me before we started dating, but I just had to have him. We met while I was a freshman in college, but I was not trying to date anybody seriously. Getting my education was my first priority, so I became the queen of friendships. Everybody was my friend.

Herbert, the sophomore who worked in the University Center cafeteria and hooked me up with free food every day, was just my friend. Shellie Foster, my roommate, tried to persuade me to give him some.

"Girl, you need to get with Herbert. You know he likes you. He's always hooking you up."

"Just because a man gives you food every day is no reason to give up the panties. Besides, he has a girlfriend back home in Austin, and I'm not looking to be anybody's fuck buddy. That's just my friend."

"Whatever, girl!!! Excuses, excuses."

Chandler, the resident assistant who had a mutual love of music and grade-B movies, was just my friend. Yet, Shellie badgered me into trying to make the relationship more than what it was.

"You know you and Chandler are meant to be together. He's always talking about you and hanging out with you. He even took you home to meet his mother. What's up with that?"

"I can't date him; that's my friend. Besides, I know too much of his business. He's goes to the club every Saturday and passes out business cards that say 'Chandler Warren, Attorney-at-Law'."

"What?"

"Yes, girl! Ain't that some crazy mess? A brother will do anything just to get some. I love him like a little brother, but he's too goofy to date. Besides, I think he's gay."

"Yeah, right. You're just saying that because you ain't gettin none!"

Larry, my study partner in Human Sexuality who always made sure to take notes for me when I missed class, was just my friend. Again, Shelly tried to maneuver a hook-up.

"Girl, Larry is FIIINNNEEE! I know you are using him as a lab partner in that Human Sexuality class. If you're not, you're crazy. I'd let him hit it every night!"

"Hell no! Larry is *married*. He tried to hit it, but I called his house one night to get the notes from class, and his wife answered the damn phone. Anyway, his toes are jacked up, and he's always wearing sandals. I could never get with him. That's just my friend."

I was satisfied with the friendship role. I amplified every fault or problem a man had in order to protect myself. It was my shield, but Nathan quickly tore it down.

We met at a Kappa party at the University Center. He was working the door with his frat brothers taking tickets when I arrived at the party with Shellie and Lisa. I always saw him around campus, but I tried not to pay any attention to him because the playboy image just did not suit me although the Kappas did throw the best parties and hosted meaningful community service programs. Most of the members were extremely popular, intelligent, and handsome–a lethal combination at any age but especially on a college campus; consequently, getting pussy was not a problem for any of them. The Kappas made the most of a prime opportunity, and Nathan was no exception to the rule.

At the door of the UC, Nathan turned on the Kappa charm, and I was not immune.

"I know you're going to dance with me." He just came right out with it. There was no sense in beating around the bush. He knew what he wanted, and he went for it.

"Sure."

"I'm serious, girl. I wanna dance with you before you leave tonight."

"Okay, whatever. Can I *please* get in the party now?"

He let us in the door, but before we could get up the stairs that led to the dance floor, Shellie and Lisa started in on me.

"Girl, he was cute."

"What's wrong with you? Why are you always playing hard to get?"

I answered them both with, "He was just flirting to be flirting. He wants a little bit more than I'm giving. I'm not trying to go out like that."

Shellie might have been fooled, but Lisa wasn't hearing it. She had known me all my life and could read my expressions just as well as my family.

"You need to stop trippin'. You know you like him. I could read it all over your face, and at least he looks better than that black ass Kyle."

I was mortified. I'm sure Nathan heard every word of our conversation since he was standing at the bottom of the stairs on which we were ascending. I sort of laughed and tried to play it off by saying, "Lisa, why are you always dissin' dark-skinned brothers! Something's wrong with your crazy ass." Then, I hurried them into the party before they could embarrass me any further.

Lisa was right about one thing. Nathan did look good. He had big brown eyes and soft black hair. He stood about ten inches above my 5'4" frame and his regular participation in intramural football made his body bulge with muscles.

As we entered the ballroom, we couldn't help but notice that the party was off the hook. The Kappas were having their regional convention in Arlington, and all of their frat brothers from the Dallas-Fort Worth area were in attendance. All of the sororities and fraternities were strutting around the dance floor, and hordes of people were in the center getting their groove on to a song by Montell Jordan.

I was feeling the music and enjoying myself when I felt a tap on my shoulder. Nathan wanted his dance, and I had no problem giving it to him. Just as we started moving, the song changed to R. Kelly's *My Body's Callin'*. I found out later that Nathan requested this song specifically for me. I stiffened, terrified of the implications. I had no problem dancing with Nathan to a fast song but a slow jam was another story. I knew my body, and I also knew that Nathan would have no problem figuring out that my body was calling–*for him*.

He put his arm around my waist, and we started to sway. We moved pelvis to pelvis, and I felt heat emanating between our bodies. Nathan towered above me, so my head was resting against his chest. I could hear the faint murmur of his heartbeat, and at that moment, I was gone. Way gone. I forgot about the many girls who sat in the dorm lobby complaining about how Nathan had gotten the panties and was now rehearsing for his part in *The Invisible Man* (you know the disappearing act men play when they're done with you). I forgot about the stories of how he used his pearly, white smile to convince some unsuspecting victim to pay his bills and buy him clothes. In that moment, everything was different. And in my mind, everything would be different about us. In Nathan's arms, I felt at ease; I felt like I was at home. Safe and secure.

We continued to dance through three more songs, but I ended the dance so I wouldn't appear desperate. It was an attempt to regain my composure; my emotions were spiraling out of control, and I needed to put them in check. That was the end of the dance, but that was not the end of Nathan.

A week later, I saw Nathan in the UC, but I quickly put my head down and pretended to be enthralled in dissecting my personal pan pizza from Pizza Hut and my *Introduction to Social Work* textbook. Nathan was not derailed. He approached my table with confidence.

"Jaslyn, right? What's up, girl?"

"Nothing. What's up with you?'

"Just looking for you. I had to ask my frat brother who you were since you left the party so early."

"I was wondering how you knew my name. Anyway, who is your frat brother, and how does he know who I am?"

"You know Solomon. I believe you two have a class together."

"Oh yeah! We have Astrology together. You know me, but I have no idea who you are. What was your name again?"

"You're going to play me like that?" Nathan was laughing because we were both aware that I knew exactly who he was. He stared at me with that infamous smile, but I refused to give in. He was being presumptuous and cocky, so I shrugged my shoulders as if I had no clue.

"My name is Nathan. Nathan Embry," he stated with confidence.

As I got up to leave, I said, "Nice to meet you, Nathan. Please, tell Solomon I said hello." And then, I left.

When I reached my dorm room, my conscience became involved in a familiar war. I resorted to my familiar pattern of overanalyzing every situation instead of dealing with the situation before me. *One of the finest men on campus could not possibly be interested in me. He must have needed a study partner or something. Instead of just asking me, he felt that it was necessary to flirt.* I put the debate in the back of my mind as my phone began to ring. It gave two short rings instead of two long ones, so I knew someone was calling me from the phone outside the dorm's entry.

"Jaslyn, this is Nathan. Meet me downstairs."

At that moment, I decided to stop dissecting all the details and go with the flow. It was what it was, and nothing more. I gave a quick okay and headed for the lobby.

When I got downstairs, Nathan was already indoors waiting with a huge grin on his face. Taking advantage of my momentary feelings of bravery, I spoke first.

"You work pretty fast! You must be stalking me...should I call campus security?"

"Nope. I'm not a stalker. I'm just resourceful. I just wanted to see if you wanted to go for some ice cream."

"I just ate lunch."

"I know. Thought you might want dessert." He grinned at me, and I shook my head laughing, but agreed to go.

We rode to Braum's Ice Cream Parlor in silence. I was definitely paranoid. The bravery that I had recently shown was definitely gone. I just knew Nathan had some psycho girlfriend who would appear at any moment and kick my ass for riding in *her* car with *her* man. He, on the other hand, was just trying to be cool.

We pulled into the parking lot. He got out of the car and came to my side to open the door. He was really pouring it on thick.

"Why all the formality? It's only ice cream, and it's not like we're on a real date."

"It's called being a gentleman in all situations, and who says we're not on a real date?" He winked at me to let me know that he knew exactly what he was doing. He also knew that it was working. As a matter of fact, it was working very well.

Inside the store, Nathan asked me what I wanted and took the liberty of ordering me a scoop of chocolate almond and a pint of buttered pecan for himself. The ice cream must have had a recipe for courage because I decided to be brave again and put my mind at ease. I was never one for being coy and hints just did not work on me. If a guy wanted to date me, then he needed to come right out and say that (I guess Kyle had spoiled me). Nathan's actions were speaking volumes, but his mouth wasn't saying a damn thing so I decided to help him along.

"Nathan, what is the deal? Why do you have me here? Don't you have a girlfriend or something?"

"No, I do not have a girlfriend, or I would not be here with you."

"Being here with me does not mean a thing. You might just want to hang out or something, and I'm not down for any crazy ass bullshit."

"Ooh! What a potty mouth we have. You know that's not very attractive for a lady to talk like that, don't you?"

"Whatever. Stop trying to avoid the issue. Besides, you asked me out not the other way around so if you don't like my mouth, then just take me back to the dorm."

"I'm not that turned off by it…and I already answered your question. I do not have a girlfriend. What type of bullshit are you talking about?"

"Like some girl coming out of nowhere accusing me of fucking her man. I've heard the stories about you."

"Stories. What stories? Wait a minute…I thought you didn't know who I was?

I was cold busted, but I tried to pull it together. "I said I didn't know your name. I've been hearing stories about Nathan Embry, but I had never seen your face. So when you said your name, I put the face with it."

"Yeah, whatever." We both laughed because the black population at UTA was very small; Nathan knew that I was lying.

I put my hand on my hip and tilted my face upwards as I looked Nathan in the eyes and tried to regain control of the conversation. "That is not the issue at hand. Stop avoiding the question!"

"I don't have a girlfriend or significant other, so you don't have to worry about someone coming out of the woodwork and clowning us. That should answer the question. Furthermore, we are not fucking, but that could change if you want it to."

I couldn't contain my laughter. I laughed so hard I dropped my ice cream. I held my side as tears rolled down my face. Nathan was furious.

"What the fuck is so funny?"

"Look who has the potty mouth now!" I gasped as I tried to catch my breath from laughing so hard. "You're funny for thinking that after a dance and some ice cream that I would even consider *kissing* you, never mind fucking you. Please! You can take me home now."

"You know what Jaslyn, you're not ready for me. I really like you, and you're trying to play with me. For your information, I was only kidding about fucking. I was simply trying to get to know you and spend time with you, but you're too immature to handle a man like me. You're too busy listening to rumors. At least I tried to get to know you before I judged you. You didn't even afford me that pleasure. I see now that you have the infamous AT-TI-TUDE!"

I sobered up long enough to try and make things right with Nathan. I was embarrassed because my maturity had been called into question. Really, I just didn't want Nathan to think he could get the upper hand so easily.

"My mother always told me that where there is smoke, there is always a fire. Now, you can call me immature if you want to, but I always listen to my mother. She hasn't lied to me yet. And what attitude? I don't have an attitude."

"You know the infamous "black girl attitude." The one where women try to tell you off for no reason or jump to conclusions and act like they don't need anyone or anything."

"I didn't mean to come across like that. You must admit that asking me to fuck on the first date is a bit presumptuous, kidding or not. I don't like to play games like that, and I don't give it up that easily, just in case you're wondering," I eyed Nathan suspiciously as I explained the situation. If he was going to pursue me then, he needed to know that I wouldn't be knocking boots with him anytime soon. Despite Shellie's best efforts to fix me up, I was still a virgin, and I planned on staying that way. I was unaware that Nathan already knew this about me and viewed me as a challenge. His hooded eyes didn't reveal any of his plans, just his obvious interest.

He smiled at my feeble attempt at an apology, "Even though it didn't sound like one, your apology is accepted. Let's just change the subject, okay?"

"Cool."

We both laughed and continued our "date." I realized he was easy to talk to and was very intelligent. His major was music and he planned to run his own nightclub some day. He was well-versed in current affairs, specifically the Clarence Thomas/Anita Hill case which was a hot topic at the time. He gained major cool points for being able to discuss racial profiling which was just coming on the scene but was of interest to me. Nathan and I also shared a love of sports, art, music (especially jazz), and watching every new movie that came to the theater. What I didn't realize about Nathan was that he had an uncanny ability to manipulate situations to his advantage. Like his ability to use my gullible nature to turn our conversation around.

Since it was the end of the spring semester and summer was approaching, UTA would be having their weekly outdoor movie festival the following Thursday. Nathan and I made a date to see the movie together, an excellent choice since it would allow both of us to do something we enjoyed and talk at the same time. It was outside, so normal movie theater rules did not apply, and we could take time to get to know each other. Besides, it was free. And on my Pell Grant budget, there wasn't too much else I could afford to do other than chill out in the dorms, which eventually led to sex…and I wasn't having that.

That movie led to a four-year relationship that was unbelievably trying. My intuition told me to run from Nathan. To run fast and hard, but in the back of my mind, I still toyed with the idea that love was possible. Maybe, this was *the* "Mr. Right" that Lloyd was talking about. I was still longing to be loved even though I had been avoiding it.

Falling in love with Nathan was easy, but falling out of love with him was very difficult and emotionally painful. While dating Nathan, I became a person I said I would never be; I did things I said I'd never do. Love will do that to you sometimes. It allowed me to let my guard down and let Nathan in. Both were huge mistakes

Chapter 7
Conversation Rules the Nation

Jaslyn: The Relationship, The Next Four Years

Nathan, Nathan, Nathan. Lord, I don't know what got into me when I decided to sleep with him. It was awful. If you didn't already know–pretty boys do not equal pretty sex! As a matter of fact, it can be quite *UGLY!* Even though Nathan was my first sexual experience and I had no one to whom I could compare him, messing around with Kyle on the front porch taught me enough to know that sex should not be like watching paint dry.

My sister Melissa married a guy named Damon. Most of the time Damon and I don't get along because he's a wannabe pimp who tries to treat my sister like shit. I was a senior in high school when they got married around 1991, so I tolerated his bullshit because I was young and I didn't know any better. Besides, he was the father of my twin nieces, so I tried to cut the brother some slack. While trying to secretly brag on his ability to get women without owning up to the fact that he was cheating on my sister, he used to tell me that "conversation rules the nation." In my textbook world, I had no idea what that meant. He kindly explained that a man could get a woman to do anything he wanted as long as he could talk a good game. It wasn't that I didn't believe him. It was just that I had never encountered anyone with the skill to do it. Until, that is, I met Nathan.

He had *mad game* and I, with my naïve self, fell for it hook, line, and sinker. Everyday he would tell me how pretty and fine I was. I already knew this, but a girl always loves to feel appreciated and made to feel beautiful. He used to tell me that he loved to touch my mahogany skin. Standing over six feet tall, Nathan would scoop down and lift me off the ground just to get a hug. It was as if he were trying to envelop me. He was never crass about his affection for me the way some men from the South usually are. You know the type. The super soul brothers who were always yelling, "Damn girl, you got them baby-making hips!" It wasn't like that with Nathan. He respected my body, although he admired it openly; he did so in a way that made me feel proud and sexy.

Nathan talked, and I was definitely listening. I was committed to my abstinence, but he was wearing me down. Using just the right amount of charm and innocence, he would tell me how much he wanted to be with me and how much he cared about me. "You can trust me. I've never wanted anyone as much as I want you." And eventually, when nothing else worked, "I want to be with you because I love you." True, I was being fed the same crap that most girls were being fed, and it worked on me as it worked on most girls. I was strong, but I wasn't superhuman.

I know, I know. How can I be so stupid? I don't know. I just know that it worked. Besides, I wanted to see what all the girls in the dorms were talking about. Sitting up listening to sex stories all night always made me feel like I was missing out on something.

The big day finally happened on a chilly day in November. We had been dating exclusively for six months, so this was our excuse to celebrate. Nathan had done a superb job setting the scene for a romantic interlude. A candlelit dinner, soft music, and fire crackling lightly in the fireplace. The lights were low, and the fire made the room feel warm and toasty. The mood was set for intimacy and seduction. His roommate was out of town, so we had the entire apartment to ourselves.

We ate our dinner, and afterward, we sat down on the sofa in front of the fireplace talking and listening to music. We talked about our goals in life and our future together. Well, Nathan talked, and I mostly listened. I was so nervous and aroused that I was tongue-tied and trembling. I knew what was about to happen. I wanted it to happen, but like always, there was a voice inside my head telling me that it was wrong. I ignored the warning because I had always lived on the side of caution, yet now, I wanted to jump in head first and experience life uninhibited. Nathan convinced me that we were in love and together, we could conquer the world. Despite clues to the contrary—he did not have a job and could not see one single project through to completion, I was still in school, and we could not maintain a conversation for more than thirty minutes without having an argument–I decided to throw caution to the wind and give myself over completely to the man that I loved.

We started kissing and caressing. My mind was already racing from the effects of the fire, food, music, and wine. I told Nathan that I wanted to go the bedroom.

"You what?"

"Let's go to the bedroom. I want to be with you."

"Are you serious?"

"Of course, I'm serious."

"You don't have to…you know that, don't you? I can wait until you're ready. I love you already, so when it happens, it will just be like icing on the cake."

He knew exactly what to say because I was convinced even more that Nathan was the man for me.

"I'm ready," I said.

We entered the bedroom, and that's where the story ends. There's nothing to it really; there's no way to even romanticize it. We got started, and then, it was over. Case closed. The entire time I was thinking that I had to get up early for work the next day. He was up there huffing and grunting, and it was hot. He didn't even try to involve me in the process. My enjoyment just didn't matter. He kissed me one time during the whole ordeal and paid no attention to any other parts of my body other than placing his penis in my vagina. What a waste of five minutes!

I stayed with him thinking that it would get better. I thought it was my fault because I was a virgin, and I didn't know what I was doing. I reasoned that the next time we had intercourse would be better because I could participate more, and I would learn what needed to be done. After our fourth time together, I told myself that sex wasn't everything.

Our relationship lasted throughout my stay in undergrad. Nathan graduated before I did, so he should have entered the workforce before me, as well. He didn't. He refused to get a job saying that he was writing a business plan and gathering investors for his club. Whenever I would ask him anything about the "investors," he would somehow manage to start an argument and avoid the issue. I didn't let it bother me too much because his bills were always paid, and he never needed anything. As a matter of fact, he was the life of the party. Blowing money on his friends and financing keg parties at the frat house. Saving money was not a concern he seemed to have.

I soon realized that he was able to stay in his apartment and keep his car because his parents paid for everything. His father called one day after receiving the Visa bill and explained that after a year of having a degree and no job nor any tangible proof of a business plan, he was cutting him off. "Grow up!" was the last thing Nathan's dad said to him before he slammed the phone down in his face. He didn't get the hint.

Eventually, he started borrowing money from me. My work-study job and Pell grant money only paid so much. I would lend him most of the money I had and I would have to scrape up the rest to pay for my expenses for school. He constantly told me, "Baby, when we get married, you'll get your money back and then some." But, the real trouble started when I urged him to get a real job. He was not amused.

"Damn, get off my back! I can't work at a regular job. I need to be my own boss. I can't spend the rest of my life working for the man. I need your support, not your criticism. Black women are always putting their men down, and then, they wonder why we say they have attitudes." This would work for a few weeks until I asked him about it again, and he came up with another excuse. He always knew exactly what to say.

Two years passed, and nothing changed. The week of my graduation I had a talk with Nathan. He had to get his shit together, or we were through. I spent most of my childhood being poor, and I was not trying to get married and continue the tradition if I could help it.

"Look, Jaslyn, I know that you have been extremely patient. Just hold on a little longer, okay. I've got this deal in the works that will set us up for life."

"It's not drugs, is it?" I hated drug dealers more than I hated the unemployed.

"No! I have an investor who's willing to put up the money for my club. All I have to do is meet with them one final time this weekend, and the deal will be closed. I can open the club and start earning some real money."

He was my man, and I wanted to support him, so I caved in one more time. "Alright, just do what you have to do, but I hope your meeting does not clash with my graduation. You've known for two months that I graduate this weekend. If you miss it, I'm going to kick your ass."

"Baby, calm down. I would not miss your graduation for anything in the world."

I graduated on a Saturday afternoon in May. Afterward, I met my friends and family in front of Texas Hall to celebrate. Mama, Carol, Francine, Melissa, Damon, Shellie, and Lisa. Everyone was there but Nathan.

It was about four in the afternoon when the commencement exercises were over, so they decided to celebrate by taking me out for an early dinner. When I returned to my dorm room, it was eight o'clock in the evening. I called Nathan but he didn't answer. I was truly pissed, so I went over to his apartment to see what happened. I opened the door with the spare key he gave me. It was no big deal. He gave me a key after we had been dating for two months, so I was used to coming and going as I pleased. His apartment reminded me of the first time we had sex–soft music, dinner, and instead of the fireplace, Nathan had the place lit up with scented candles. The smell of vanilla and jasmine permeated the air. He hadn't done this for me since our first time, so I immediately became excited. *He must have done this as a surprise for my graduation*, I thought. Here I was ready to crucify the poor man for being thoughtless, and the entire time he was going to surprise me. I had already forgiven him when I ran to the bedroom and threw open the door.

It was like being in a dream, an alternate universe, the fifth dimension, or some fantastic crap like that because the shit was unreal. I must have been hallucinating. I wanted to be hallucinating. Nathan had some white girl on all fours pumping the shit out of her ass.

I wailed. Like a wolf howling at the moon. That's the only way I can explain it. When they heard me and saw the look on my face, Snow White ran straight for the corner, hid behind a chair, and started yelling, "Please don't hurt me. Please don't hurt me!" I stopped crying long enough to pay closer attention. I blinked and took a better look. She had long, dark hair and pale, pink skin. Just like in the fairy tale. But the there was a difference. She sounded like RuPaul. Snow White was a man. Nathan was fucking a damn man.

I looked at him, and his punk ass ran for the bathroom. Before he could get there, I grabbed a lamp from a table next to the door and threw it at the back of his head. It hurled him against the wall as it hit its mark. He moaned and started crawling for the door like a soldier wounded in combat. I jumped on his back and commenced to putting a beat down on his ass. Slapping, scratching, and punching. I tried with all my might to kill the bastard.

"You sorry piece of shit!" Nathan's football skills came in handy because he flipped me off of him and pinned me to the ground.

"It's not what you think! He's giving me money for the club!"

"So you're a gay now?!" I screamed while trying to free myself from his grasp. "He sucked your dick? No, I get it. You sucked his dick first, then you fucked him in the ass. Fuck you and fuck the club! Get the hell up off me!!"

"Not until you calm down! Jaslyn, please calm down."

At this point Snow White yells from the corner, "Don't let her up, she'll kill me!"

"Shut up, bitch!! Ain't nobody thinking about you. I know who my problem's with. This sorry piece of shit on top of me. LET ME UP RIGHT NOW!" I was kicking and screaming, wanting so bad for him to hurt physically the way I was hurting emotionally.

"Not until you promise to calm down, and promise me that you will stop hitting me or anybody else for that matter."

I took a deep breath, which only made the tears come down harder, which only made me angrier, which only made me want to hit him more. But, I was determined to leave because, more than anything, I hated for him to see me cry. So, I said, "Let me up. I won't hit you anymore."

"You promise."

I raised my hand in Scout's Honor and said, "Now, would you *please* get the fuck up off me?"

He let me up, and I left the apartment. But, I wasn't through. Once I made it to the parking lot, I headed straight for my car. I popped the trunk and took the tire iron out. Then, I went in the back seat and went in my purse to retrieve the box cutter that I used for protection

I found Nathan's car and finished what I started. When I was done, not one window was left nor was there any air left in one tire. Finally, I left a message on the hood for all the women who might even consider hooking up with him. "DON'T FUCK WITH DICK SUCKIN' HOES!!!"

I made it home, but the campus police were waiting on me. Nathan and Snow White were looking out the window as I completed my artwork. They called 911, and when a white person calls the police in the south, they don't hesitate to show up. Instead of getting my groove on at the club *or* in the bedroom, I spent my graduation night in the Ott Cribbs Jail in downtown Arlington for assault and vandalism.

Nathan's bitch ass had also told them about the fight in his bedroom, and he had the scratches and the white boy to prove it. I couldn't even be mad anymore. As I sat in jail, all I could do was cry, lamenting the death of my innocence and welcoming the birth of a woman scorned.

Chapter 8
An Around The Way Girl

Contrary to what you probably believe, Alicia didn't derail my pursuit of other girls. As a matter of fact, it did just the opposite. I pursued them with a vengeance. To borrow a phrase from my dear friend Malik, I like to refer to it as a youthful period of validation. It was as if the more girls I dated, then that provided further evidence that Alicia was a fool for dissin' me the night of the prom. I was a male tease. I spent quality time with my female friends, doing my best to make them feel that they were God's gift, but the moment they wanted to get emotionally close to me; I didn't hesitate to move on. I didn't allow myself to become sexually involved with anyone. I still believed that Uncle Junior's sexual escapades were the sole reason my Aunt Tootie was unhappy, so I refused to dog a girl out like that. To be honest with you, this was the late eighties, and HIV was on a rampage, so I made a conscious effort to save my life the best way I could. Hold Out. You can call me a punk if you want to, but I did what I had to do.

I chose to treat women right, as best I could, without becoming emotionally close. My defense mechanism worked well at the time, but as I look back, I was no better than Uncle Junior. I was an emotional whore. Using women to make me feel good about myself until they invested their feelings, and then, I moved on to the next girl so she could prove how great I was again. I didn't know that then; I know it now…hindsight *is* 20/20.

During my senior year, one girl brought me to my knees. She was the type of girl that wouldn't allow you to tiptoe around her heart. You had to come with something real with her, or you needed to move on. Her name was Asia Brooks, and she was what we used to call an around-the-way girl."

I would be leaving for college in a matter of months, and I had started to feel like it was time for me to get serious about life. I began to seriously contemplate settling down; doing so with a girl from home seemed practical since the college I would be attending was in Denton, which was only forty-five minutes away from home. I reasoned that this would be the perfect scenario with any girlfriend because we would be far enough away from each other to not get on one another's nerves but close enough so that I could still spend time with her.

It was time for me to navigate my life onto its proper course: college, job, house, and wife. I didn't want to spend the next five years of my life trying to figure out who my wife would be, so it seemed efficient to find her first. All of my friends now had steady girlfriends, and it seemed right for me to have one as well. *Yes, peer pressure is a bitch!*

I used to hang out with Jawaan and Malik at Echo Lake each Sunday afternoon. It was a man-made lake on the Southside of the city. A mile of road encircled the lake, which made it possible for you to enter on the north side of the lake and exit on the south side or vice versa. It was the perfect place for families because it had a baseball field, a playground that included a merry-go-round, a swing set, and a slide. The ducks would walk right up to you and eat bread from your hand. To a kid from the ghetto, Echo Lake represented the perfect example of a Norman Rockwell painting—Monday through Thursday. Weekends, however, were another story.

Echo Lake became a den for every African-American teenager in the city of Fort Worth looking for something to do on a Sunday afternoon. It was our time to showcase, hang out, and socialize. The lake became congested with hundreds of adolescents trying to demonstrate how cool they were by standing around, talking, drinking, and parading through the lake in Regals, Cadillacs, and Mustangs. And if you didn't have a sports car, you had to make sure that the one you rolled in was washed and waxed, and that the rims or hubcaps glistened like diamonds on a rapper's chain. The music blasted at the highest decibels from the time we got there until the police came to break up the action.

The Southside was not our preference to hang out, but the fellas and I chose to go to Echo Lake on Sundays because of the plethora of girls to choose from. Sycamore Park, which was closer to Stop Six, was the chosen location on Saturdays.

It was the weekend of spring break, and every Black teenager in Tarrant County was at the lake looking for something to do. We arrived in Jawaan's car because Malik didn't have a car, and I was not about to cruise Echo Lake in my Chevy Chevette. Jawaan's 1989 Escort wasn't the most expensive car, but it was clean and reliable. He had it tricked out with rims, a fresh paint job, tinted windows, and 808 speakers in the trunk. We decided to park next to the playground. The three of us leaned against the side of the car to show off our acid washed jeans and Adidas sneakers–a prime opportunity to check out the women, to show off Jawaan's car, and to sport our new clothes.

We scanned the area, trying to determine which girls were the finest, the prettiest, and the easiest to approach when I spotted a girl standing with a group of her friends. The group seemed to be involved in an intimate conversation with about four or five guys who were cruising the lake in a Cutlass.

At first, I wasn't attracted to her because she was wearing a popular hairstyle at the time that I detested– DOOKIE BRAIDS. Ugh! She was a bonified around-the-way girl." How did LL Cool J put it? "A girl with extensions in her hair, bamboo earrings, at least two pair." With further inspection, however, she became more attractive. She had the long legs and butterscotch skin that I was so fond of, but as I eavesdropped on her conversation, she also had a modicum of intelligence that was a must in any woman I dated. I was sold.

I wanted to approach her, but I knew better than to walk up to a man's car and try to run game on a girl that he was talking to. In Texas, that was grounds for a fight. I wasn't down with that–I could throw down with the best of 'em, but I liked to spread love, not war. I decided to wait. There was the chance that I might miss my opportunity if she chose to get in the car with him, but by the way the conversation was going, the brother wasn't that smart. With a girl like this, you at least needed to be able to conjugate a verb. He wasn't that successful.

Malik spotted who I was looking at and started tripping.

"Man, are you looking at Asia?" He seemed baffled by my choice. I knew what he was talking about but I played dumb.

"Who is Asia?"

"The girl in the Guess jeans you've been eyeing since we got here. The one talking to the guys in the Cutlass."

"Oh, her! Yeah, I'm checking her out. What about it?"

"Sam, you don't want to fool with that girl. She's got a shitty attitude, and she's broke as hell. She's my cousin. Now if I say that about her and she's family, then you know something's wrong."

"Malik, you think all women have shitty attitudes, and I am not a male gold digger like you and Jawaan. She has a shitty attitude with you. She doesn't even know me, and I'm not trying to get with her for her money."

"Well, what are you trying to get with her for? It's the booty. Oops, my bad. I forgot you were still a virgin, so we know that's not the reason!"

"DAAAMMMNNN!!" That was Jawaan and every other dude standing around.

I was about to jump in Malik's ass, but at that very moment, Asia walked away from the Cutlass and headed towards the playground. I saw my opportunity, but I was not sure how to seize it because anger at Malik clouded my judgment.

She and her friends headed toward the car next to ours. Malik sensed my urgency and came to the rescue. He didn't approve of my choice, but he was still my boy; he would always look out for me.

"Hey, Asia! What's going on girl?"

"Malik, why are you talking to me? You know I don't like you!"

"Damn, we are cousins! I was just speaking. What the hell is your problem?"

"Distant cousins. Don't confuse yourself. I still don't like you. I hate men like you and your silly friends who objectify women."

My anger at Malik dissipated as I saw an opportunity to engage her in verbal warfare.

"First of all…Asia, right?"

"Yessss," she dragged out the s and rolled her eyes to emphasize her attitude.

"Asia, just like women, men hate to be grouped together or stereotyped. Second, if you don't want to be objectified, then why are you at Echo Lake on a Sunday, when every thug and his mama are hanging out, walking around in those tight-ass jeans? It's because you *want* men to look at you. Finally, it didn't help your image or the cause of feminism to see you and your crew hanging out the side of a car that was packed with a bunch of wannabe pimps. Are you not participating in your own objectification?"

I was feeling myself. I knew that by standing up to her I had a chance. She had a strong personality, and weak men would not fare well on her love barometer.

Everyone in earshot had tuned in for my reply and was now prepared to witness the show that I didn't know was coming.

"Let me tell you something…" she said searching for my name.

"Sam."

"Let me tell you something, Sam. I was not talking to you."

"But you were referring to me."

"I repeat. I. Was. Not. Talking. To. You."

I had not learned yet that I would never win in a battle of wits with a woman. I repeated my attempt to debate her. "Again, I…"

She cut me off. "I was *not* finished. I let you finish what you had to say. Now, I'm going to finish.

"I was not talking to you. How do you know that I included you in that group of silly friends? I would hope that

Malik has more than two friends…but, you're right, his sorry behind probably doesn't.

"Since I didn't call names and you were the first to speak up, what does that say about you? Are you guilty? Have you ever heard that when you kick a dog, he will holler? Well, I guess I kicked you pretty hard.

"In this country, a woman can wear what she wants to wear. That's not a crime, but staring at a woman's behind, if not a crime, is in the very least offensive. So, stop staring at my ass! You had to be doing it to know that my jeans are tight. Finally, why is it that when a girl is talking to someone in a car, people automatically assume she is flirting or tricking? That might have been my brother, which, for your information, it was.

"Again, I wasn't talking to you. So you need to think twice before you jump into other people's conversations."

A round of oohs and damns rang out from the crowd. Black people in Fort Worth loved to instigate.

Before I could respond, Malik chimed in with, "Girl, you know that wasn't yo' damn brother!" Everyone burst out laughing, including Asia and myself. The tension had been broken, and we were given an out to save face. The fact that she could laugh about the whole situation made me more attracted to her, so I ignored my initial reaction to her braids and considered getting to know her.

Our first date was the typical high school outing, dinner and a movie. Working with my Dominos' Pizza paycheck, this was all I could afford, but it was not really conducive for stimulating conversation.

I picked her up in my Chevette, a product of my job at Domino's. It was not really a chick magnet, but I was still proud of it. We proceeded to the theater first, and since it was a horror flick, one of those Jason movies I believe, we had a legitimate excuse for premature cuddling.

The movies led to a late dinner on a Saturday evening. Asia was extremely bright and even more attractive in the soft light of the restaurant. The fact that she had removed those hideous braids and let her natural light brown hair flow to her shoulders was an added bonus. That's where I started the conversation.

"What happened to your braids?"

"Oh, I took those out. It was just an experiment that I let my friend talk me into. I'm not really into synthetic hair."

"Oh."

"Why? Didn't you like them?"

"No, that's not it. I was just asking."

"You can be honest. I won't get mad."

"Well, now that you mention it, no I didn't like them."

She laughed while saying, "I'm glad you told the truth because if you had lied this date would have been over."

"How would you have known if I had lied or not?"

"I just would have…I knew the first answer was a lie."

"Oh, really?"

"Really," she declared confidently.

"Well, I'm glad I told the truth then."

We continued talking over chicken strips and root beer. I tried to keep the banter light, but somehow, the topic of sex managed to enter into our conversation.

"I heard you used to date Mona Washington from Dunbar"

"Who told you that?"

"Don't worry about who told me, just answer the question. Did you date Mona or not?"

"Well, since you are all up in my business, investigating a brother, we went out a few times, but it was nothing serious.'

"Did you have sex with her?"

"Damn, girl! You get straight to the point, don't you?

"Yes."

"What's the deal? Do you have something against Mona?"

"Nothing. She's just a hoe, that's all."

"I am definitely not feeling the love up in here! What did she do to you to deserve that?'

"Nothing. I don't even know her. She has a reputation for sleeping with any and everybody, and I don't want to sleep with anyone who came close to that. You know AIDS kills."

"True. But, who said that *we* were going to sleep together? Is there something you want to tell me?" I winked at her.

"You don't want to go there with me."

"That's where you're wrong. I do want to go there, and I want to get there as soon as possible."

"Huh! You think you're cute, don't you?"

"I know it, and I hope you do, too!"

"I hope you don't think that I am going to have sex with you tonight because I'm not like that.'

"Like what?'

"Don't play dumb; you know what I mean."

"I probably do, but why don't you enlighten me?"

"I mean that I am not easy. I don't give it up on the first date."

"So, do you give it up on the second date?" My grin told her that I was playing but would take the opportunity if given the chance.

"You know what, let's just end this conversation because I can see where it's going."

"Hey, you brought it up not me. That's what you get for being all up in my business."

"Okay, okay. You got me."

With a straight face I asked her, "But seriously, will you give it up on the second date?"

We both laughed. She only responded with, "Shut up, Sam!"

I knew I had her when she laughed. I entered her comfort zone and had become familiar to her.

Asia exhibited a raw sex appeal that was irresistible. I was glad that I decided to take a chance with her. She became more appealing to me every time I talked to her.

The thing about dating an around-the-way girl is that you have to stay on your p's and q's. It is not an easy job and not a job meant for the average brother. Homegirls, as they are often referred to, look for men with goals and ambitions. You must actively pursue them. They want a man to demonstrate the utmost respect for them, but at the same time, they want a man with a backbone. Someone who is sensitive to their needs but who won't hesitate to put them in check when they get out of line. I'm proud to say that I held down my job pretty well.

Dating her was a relief; I could relax a little bit because there wasn't the pressure of trying to be someone I wasn't. I didn't have to be ashamed of my family situation because Asia's family wasn't a candidate for an episode of *Leave it Beaver,* either. She lived in the Butler Housing Projects near downtown. Her father was MIA, and her mom was a certified "Welfare Queen," refusing in any form or fashion to get a job and support her eight children. Asia and I had bonded on a deeper level than I had with most girls. She had been where I had been and seen what I had seen. Like me, she was motivated to move beyond her circumstances, despite seemingly insurmountable odds. Asia was the first girl to make me question my decision to remain a virgin. It was probably due to the fact that I felt a strong connection with her, but whatever the reason, I was ready to move beyond the realm of friendship to that of lovers. I knew that Asia was the person to do it with.

I was a virgin, but she was not. Yet, according to her, she loved sex but was very particular about who she chose to sleep with. We never really got into many details about it because I trusted her.

Jawaan and Malik didn't really bother me too much about my decision to remain abstinent. They knew my stance and respected my decision; although, they didn't necessarily agree with it, especially Malik who slept with girls like they were test dummies for Sealy Posturepedic.

As my relationship with Asia deepened, I sensed some hesitation from my friends who always tried to have my back.

One day, they broached the subject while we were playing basketball at school. We were outside shooting hoops on the blacktop. I was standing against the fence surrounding the blacktop taking a break to catch my breath when Jawaan attempted to see just how deep my feelings for Asia were.

"Yo, Sam. Can I holla at you about something?"

"Yeah, man. What's up?" I was confused. I thought he might want to borrow some money or something. He had just quit his job at the grocery store to spend more time with his family before he left for school. I didn't want him to worry because Jawaan had been there for me during the most difficult times in my life, and I would do anything for him. He was an amiable and jovial person. He never let life's problems worry him and he always seemed to let everything roll off his shoulders, but on this day, he seemed pensive. I knew he was treading cautiously.

"What's up with you and Asia?"

"We're cool."

"Just cool. Is that all?"

My heart stopped. I cared for Asia. A lot. I didn't know what to expect.

Jawaan hesitated to go on, so I urged, "What is it?"

"*Calm down!* I just wanted to see how you felt about her, that's all."

"Why?"

"Asia's just not a girl you would normally date."

"I know that, but I like her. Are you dating her? Do you like her?"

"Hell no! I would never do you like that. You're my best friend. Look, I'm just saying that Asia is…a little more worldly, that's all. Her mind isn't the only thing that she's liberated with."

"Worldly?" I didn't get his point.

Malik, who had just finished his turn on the court, walked over to us and joined in the conversation. He was always willing to speak up and brave the accusation of being crass.

"She's a hoe, okay! A hoe." He wiped his forehead and took a drink of his water as if he had announced that it was now my turn to play.

Needless to say, I was pissed. He'd called my girlfriend a whore to my face. "Don't be jealous because the ladies love me. You know I got Cherokee in my blood!" Despite playing football and basketball, Malik was still struggling with baby fat and a slight acne problem. Jawaan and I were considered pretty boys, so most girls tried to talk to us first. Malik just normally picked up the leftovers, which he readily accepted.

Jawaan and I laughed, but Malik wasn't amused. "Yeah, man, you probably are mixed with Cherokee since there's no telling who your daddy is!" I jumped off the fence. I was going to put my foot in his ass, but Jawaan jumped between us.

"Let it go, Sam. You know he's crazy." Everyone knew about my mother's drug addiction and the numerous men she slept with to support her habit. I still didn't want to let him insult my family and get away with it, but I decided to cool it. Everyone on the court had stopped what they were doing to see what was going on. I wasn't about to let the entire school watch us fight.

"It's cool, J. I know he's lying about Asia anyway. He's a fucking liar! He's just jealous because nobody wants his fat ass!"

"Jealous. Negro, please! Nobody's jealous of you. Because you're my boy, I'm going to let that fat comment slide. Your girl has whorish tendencies, and we just wanted you to know what you were getting yourself into."

"I know Asia's not a virgin and I don't judge her for that, but she told me she's only slept with two people. Why would she lie about something like that?" They laughed. Hysterically. Again, Malik took joy in bursting my bubble.

"Boy, don't you know that girls never tell the truth about who they sleep with? Look, Sam, I know you think I hate women, but I don't. I just don't trust them. No woman is worth being trusted. Even the girls that go to church every Sunday will lie with a straight face, knowing they're the main contestants for those *Pop-that-Coochie* contests they have at the club every weekend. I know you don't believe it, but it's the truth." Malik had serious trust issues with women because after his dad left, his mother had a continuous parade of men around her kids trying her best to keep them fed and clothed. There's no telling what he saw, and he never talked about it.

Still doesn't. It just manifested itself in his attitude toward women.

I didn't want to believe him. Jawaan, again, was our voice of reason. The calm in the midst of my and Malik's storm.

"Look, do you really like this girl?" He asked me.

"Yeah, I do."

"Then keep dating her and see where it goes. Maybe she's changed. You never know."

Malik, still being Malik, had to add his two cents in, "Besides your horny ass might finally get some trim." Despite our differences, I could never stay mad at Malik. He was too damned funny.

I couldn't help but laugh as I threw the ball at his head and said, "Shut up, fool."

He caught the ball and yelled, "AAHHH, ME SO HORNY," to the tune of the infamous song by Luke.

My friends were telling me to leave Asia alone, but my feelings were saying something entirely different. I decided to stay and see where it went.

I stayed on my p's and q's, and I never disrespected Asia. If she needed anything, she knew I was just a phone call away. Those phone calls started coming more frequently as she needed clothes, shoes, and purses. Somehow, I never felt used. Probably because she always told me I was the best boyfriend she ever had. To be honest, I was proud of that, and I wanted to do everything possible to make sure it stayed that way.

Slowly, but surely we started to make out on a regular basis. I was still filled with trepidation about taking things to a higher level because Malik and Jawaan's words still rested heavily on my mind. I decided to just keep my ear to the ground for rumors about her virtue, and so far, there hadn't been any.

One Friday night, Asia and I went out on a triple date with Malik and Jawaan to celebrate our recent graduations from high school and the fact that we had received scholarships to college. I was going on an academic scholarship; having graduated as the fifth ranked person in my class, I more than deserved the money. Jawaan and Malik both went on basketball scholarships. We were elated because without this money, high school would have been the end of the educational road for us.

Asia was feeling especially generous, and I was feeling especially adventurous, so after our date we ended up at the Sunset Motel on Mansfield Highway. All I need to say is that this girl turned me out. Once she put the ice cubes in her mouth and blew on my dick, I would have been her sex slave forever. *Would have.*

About four days later while I was using the bathroom, I screamed in pain. My brother ran into the bathroom. My Aunt Tootie was at work that morning, and Uncle Junior was down at the corner store getting drunk with his friends, again. Solomon was the only one there to check on me.

"Man, what's wrong with you?"

"My dick is on fire!"

"What?"

"It's burning! It's burning!"

We looked down and this green stuff was oozing from the head. I was almost in tears. Solomon looked at me and said, "Let's go!"

He drove me to the clinic in my car. The doctor confirmed my worst fears. I had gonorrhea. I knew who gave it to me.

I thought about the night we had sex. I remembered that I only brought two condoms with me, thinking that if I got lucky, I could get a second stab at Asia. I used one of the condoms in the parking lot before we even got out of the car. The girl was a freak. People were walking by and staring but she didn't seem to care. In fact, it turned her on more–she rode the dick even harder! We used the last condom the minute we entered the room. I was satisfied, but then she tied my hands to the headboard of the bed and started sucking my dick and fondling my balls. When she was done, she untied me and told me she wanted me to hit it from the back. I explained that I was out of condoms. She could have cared less; she didn't bring any protection, and I was not about to leave to get more, so I took a chance. I was wrong. *Damn was I wrong!*

When I got home, I called Asia, ready to tell her about herself, but she had something to tell me first.

"I've been meaning to talk to you. There's just no other way to say this. I'm pregnant."

I forgot about the gonorrhea. "How in the hell do you know you are pregnant, and we only had sex four days ago?"

"I'm two months."

Asia and I had been dating for almost three months, and our first sexual encounter was only a few days ago. It was quite obvious she was not the girl she presented herself to be. I hung up the phone.

My dick was burning, and my girl was having another man's baby. One word came to my mind. SUCKER!

Chapter 9
Blindsided by Love

Sampson, 1994

I convinced myself that women weren't worthy the trouble after the fiasco with my girlfriend from college. She was really fucked up. Her name was Layla, and she was so fine that she would leave a brother at a loss for words. She had a ghetto booty. You know the kind old brothers talk about sitting a drink on top of, and she had legs that went on for days. But–there is always a "but" in these situations isn't there–she was one CRAZY BITCH!

I kind of sensed it when we first started going out, but she was fine, and I was horny, so I thought, "What the hell?" We met at open-mic night at a café in South Dallas. I was on stage performing a piece I wrote called "How Can I Be Down?". As I exited the stage, she was standing in line waiting to perform her poem. The room was dim. Soft tea lights were placed strategically on every table, and a muted stage light was aimed only at performers on the small stage. I noticed her piercing eyes staring directly at me.

As I walked by, she said, "Excuse me. Do I know you?"

"No, I don't think so."

"You look so familiar. I'm sure I've met you somewhere before. Where are you from?"

"Fort Worth."

"Oh. No, that's not it. But I do know you. Are you sure you're not from Dallas?"

"I think I would know where I was born. No, I'm not from Dallas," I said with a laugh so I would not offend her. She was pretty, and I was curious.

"Where do you go to school?"

"I'm assuming you mean college. I attend the University of North Texas."

"That's where I know you from," she exclaimed.

As I smirked, I said, "So, you really do know me. I thought you were just trying to pick me up."

She chuckled good-naturedly and said, "Don't flatter yourself, sweetheart. I'm not that desperate. But since you obviously seem to be interested, you can call me." Just as she was about to give me her number, her name was called for her to approach the stage.

Solemnly, she approached the microphone. Her head was bent, and her voice was a deep tremor. She began slowly, without using the rhythmic staccato format of most spoken word artists. She simply said what was on her mind, which added a dramatic effect to her material. She had something on her mind, and she needed to get it off. Nothing was going to prevent that. Immediately, her attitude changed from a friendly open woman to a somber girl who'd had her heart broken too many times before.

> Soft as the moonlight, bright as the sun
> Our moments together can never be undone.
> We've been together, close and yet free.
> How will we manage when love we don't see?
> You are my standard for all that a man should be
> But things go wrong because now there is no me.
> I was lost to myself, living only for you.
> I was not enough and now we are through.
> I went to a place submerged deep within
> My sanity I questioned as I reflect on the sin.
> Delilah betrayed Sampson for money not love.
> My loyalty to you drove out the sun.
> As asteroids collide, sparks fly through the air
> So did our love in a life that's not fair.

She stepped from the stage, soft and sure, yet the pain was still evident on her face. The crowd was appreciative and freely gave up snaps and claps to show the girl some love. They may not have really gotten it, but they respected the craft. I could tell by how quickly she moved she didn't really care whether anyone got it or not. It seemed that for some reason she just wanted to get the poem over with. She sat down at her table. A grave expression glued to her face.

Before she performed, Layla's self-assuredness intrigued me, but something told me she was bad news. I held my ground and waited for her to exit the stage. I decided to wait to approach her. Having just performed myself, I recognized the need to reflect on her performance. It was like having an orgasm. If it was good, you wanted to bask in the after-glow, holding on to the feeling for as long as you could. Words spoken, unprovoked movement can break the spell and ruin the mood.

After several minutes, I approached her with anticipation. I hoped she was still as interested as she seemed to be earlier.

"So you wrote a poem about me," I stuttered. Again, I was mesmerized by her beauty.

"What?" Her attitude was extremely clear. She wanted to be left alone. The girl had made a complete 180. I mean before, she was open and friendly. Hell, she was the one who approached me. Now, I sensed an evil twin lurking somewhere beneath the surface. She reminded me of a character in a movie I once saw–*Sybil*. I persisted anyway.

"The poem was about me. I'm Sampson Tate…We met in line…we attend the same university." I waited patiently between each statement for her to reply.

She looked at me and said, "And?"

Despite the cold shoulder, I wanted to get to know this girl, so I kept trying. I extended my hand for her to shake it. "Nice poem," I said.

"Thanks but it wasn't about you," she replied despondently. She didn't take my hand, so I put it down.

"I know that. I'm just trying to break the ice. I thought a little humor might do the trick. You seem a little down after your performance. You want to talk about it?"

"Not really. It's best to leave the past in the past."

"Well, I don't want to disturb you any further. I'll leave you alone."

"No. I'm sorry. I don't mean to be rude. Sampson, right? I'm Layla. Layla Malone. Nice to meet you. Please, forgive me. It was my first performance, and I just kind of zoned out."

"No problem. Layla. A beautiful name for a gorgeous woman."

"Thank you. I don't know what to say."

"Don't say anything. It's the truth. I'm just being honest. I hope you don't mind me asking, but are you here alone?"

"No."

"Oh. Maybe, it would be best if I left you alone. I don't want your boyfriend to come out the bathroom and start clowning a brother."

She laughed. "It's not like that. I came with my friend, Samantha."

"Well, you've been sitting here for half an hour by yourself. I was just wondering."

Immediately, she was taken aback. "Are you some type of pervert? Do you get off by hovering over women? "

"Hell no!" Then I tried my best to turn on the charm. "When I see a woman as beautiful as you are, I find it difficult to take my eyes off of her."

"Oh, you *are* good. You keep this up, and we'll be on our first anniversary."

I laughed. Not one to mince words, I cut to the chase. "Layla, I find you intriguing, and I would love to get to know you better. Can we meet for coffee sometime?"

"Sure. I like a man that's direct. I'm free next Saturday."

"Can I call you sometime next week to make arrangements?"

We exchanged phone numbers and talked a few more minutes.

"Layla, it was nice meeting you, and I look forward to seeing you next week."

"Thanks and so do I. By the way, Sampson, I *was* just trying to pick you up." She smiled, and I was hooked. We dated for two years. Two of the most difficult years of my life.

After our first coffee date, Layla and I were inseparable. It was instant chemistry. Sometimes, the result of a chemical equation is an explosion. As our relationship developed, the chemicals of our emotions began to heat up, and we soon reached our boiling points.

During the honeymoon of our relationship, we made love everyday. Layla was an extremely passionate and noisy lover. She would often roughly encourage me not to stop, which only served to stroke my ego, and I would try with all my might not to. Sex was not the only reason I fell for her. Layla was beyond intelligent. She loved to discuss politics (national and local). Daily, we would debate issues that affected our community and the economic status of black families. She also loved sports. All kinds. If she didn't know about it, then she wanted to learn. But her favorite was baseball, as was mine. And, she could cook. Layla stimulated my mind as well as my body. *What more could a man ask for?*

We dated for a year, found a duplex on campus, and moved in together. It was then that I realized that she never trusted me. It was subtle at first. My phone would ring, and she would ask who it was. I just thought she was nosy, not suspicious. One day, I caught her with my cell phone in her hand. I didn't think anything of it until my messages had been cleared. I let it slide.

Trust is based on knowledge. We trust or don't trust people because of our knowledge of who they are. The problem with Layla and myself was that we didn't know each other. Before we moved in together, we never really discussed previous relationships. Asia taught me that women never really told the truth about who they were, so I decided to see for myself what Layla was all about.

That was a terrible mistake. Layla had a very checkered past. I learned about it the hard way, partially through arguments. She had expectations for me based on previous relationships, expectations I knew nothing about. For instance, if I opened the door for a beautiful woman, she would accuse me of flirting.

"If you want to ask her out, just go ahead. Let me know so I can move on!"

"All I did was open the damn door! What the fuck are you trippin' about?"

"Oh, no your bitch ass didn't just curse at me. That's it. I'm sick of your cheating ass. You're starting that same shit, just like my fucking ex-boyfriend. I'm not going through this shit again!"

"What the hell? What are you talking about?"

"If you don't want to be with me, just tell me." This would go on for hours until I convinced her that I was not cheating, and I loved her. Or, I just got tired of fighting and went to sleep.

Soon, our relationship started to disintegrate. I needed some space, and I started spending more time with Jawaan and Malik. To be frank, I just wanted a break from all the drama. Every day, Layla started an argument about something small, and it always lead to her accusing me of sleeping around and lying about it.

I was tired. The only way to deal with Layla was to talk crazy to her. She was never satisfied until I called her a crazy bitch or something worse. I hated talking to her that way, but it seemed that was the only way to pacify her. As soon as my language got rough, she became a kitten purring in my hands. She would always apologize to me saying, "I'm sorry, baby. You know I love you. I don't know why I act so crazy. It's because you're so good to me. I don't want to lose you. Tell me what you want. I'll do whatever you ask." And she meant it, too. Layla would cook me a gourmet meal, run my bath, and massage my entire body. This was always followed by some hellified sex! And I took it gladly.

But, her behavior got worse when I started hanging out with Jawaan and Malik. She lost her mind with curiosity and accusations. One day, we went to play some basketball, and as soon as I walked through the door, she started nagging me.

"Where the fuck have you been?"

"Playing ball."

"Oh, so you can't call somebody and tell them where the fuck you are?!"

I remained calm. We had gone through this a million times. I was not about to let her upset me, which drove her even crazier. "First of all, stop cursing at me. I'm not your child. Second, I told you where I was going this afternoon when I left."

"That was at one o'clock. It's now five. You mean to tell me that you've been playing ball for four straight hours!"

"Yes." My calmness was like pouring alcohol in her wounds because she went berserk.

"You're lying! You are a MOTHERFUCKIN' LIAR! I hate you, Sampson. I hate your damn guts for lying so fucking much. Why don't you just tell me the truth? Huh?! Huh?!"

"Whatever, Layla. I don't have to lie to you, and, if you don't trust me, why are you still with me? Let me make a suggestion. Get a life so you don't have to keep tabs on mine all the fuckin' time!"

SMACCKK!! I blinked. My eyes saw spots, and I tried to regain my focus. Layla had slapped the shit out of me.

I grabbed Layla's shoulders ready to shake the life out of her. Just as I was about to, an image of Uncle Junior came to my mind. I left the house before I became a man I said I would never be.

I hopped in my Ford Ranger I had recently purchased and drove around the city for a while. Eventually, I called Solomon and Jawaan. I didn't call Malik because I couldn't deal with his mouth at that moment. I needed stability, and my brother and my best friend were the two people I knew that could provide that.

We met at Denny's, and I relayed the story. I told them that I was sick of Layla's accusations and that I was leaving her. Even though I would never hit her, that did not mean I was willing to become the victim myself. I was shocked at what they had to say. Solomon spoke first.

"Don't leave her. Not yet."

"What?" I was dumbfounded. *Did they not just hear me? This girl just slapped me and for no fucking reason.* Jawaan cosigned on Solomon's assessment.

"I agree. Man, you really like this girl. So, why don't you try to talk to her and see what's going on?

"Yeah," Solomon said. "She's obviously dealing with some things. If you really care about her, then try to help her through them. Don't just leave her hanging. Pray with her. Seek spiritual healing with her if you really care about her. That will show her that you can be trusted. There's no telling what type of Negroes she's used to dealing with." Solomon was a Christian, and he always found a way to talk about God and spirituality.

Although, I disagreed, I nodded my head in acquiescence. I valued their counsel and wanted to see if it worked because I really did care about Layla. I was just tired of the bullshit and the drama.

After about three or four hours, I pulled into our duplex. I approached the house full of encouragement thinking that Layla and I could really work on our relationship. But as I was going in, I realized that hope was fading fast. I saw all my belongings in trash bags sitting on the porch.

I walked in the door, and Layla was sitting in the living room on the floor crying her eyes out. I didn't want to re-ignite the flame that had set her off earlier, so I spoke slowly and deliberately.

"Why are my clothes sitting outside?"

"Right after you left, I was upset. I thought you were cheating on me so I packed up your stuff. I realized that I overreacted this afternoon and that I was wrong. I jumped to conclusions. I swore to myself that when you came home I would apologize and prove to you that I was going to change. You were gone for so long that I started thinking that maybe something bad had happened to you. You never came back so that's when I..." Her voice trailed off, and she dropped her head. That's when I noticed the empty bottle of pills sitting next to her on the floor.

I panicked. I ran to her on the floor and grabbed her shoulders. This time I did shake her.

"Layla, did you take these pills?!"

"Please don't leave me, Sam. Please don't. I'll change. I promise."

"Layla!" I shook her again. "How long ago did you take these damn pills?!"

Her speech started to slur, "I...promise...just don't...leeeaave...like...my daddy...and...all the...others..." Her daddy and what others? I didn't know what the hell she was talking about. She had never told me anything about her family or her other relationships. I realized that I really didn't know much about this girl but I seriously didn't want her dying on me.

Layla passed out, and I called 911. The ambulance came, and I rode to the hospital with her. We got there just in time, but Layla had to stay for psychiatric evaluation. When she got out of the hospital a week later, I was nowhere to be found. Malik told me he saw her at open mic night a few weeks later performing a poem about how I tried to kill her.

I told you that girl was crazy!!!!

Chapter 10
Lorenzo

Jaslyn, 1999

I know I left you all hanging about Lorenzo but I had to take a break from all the redundant bullshit with Nathan. Just thinking about that sorry, pseudo-black man still makes my stomach turn. Anyway, I digress. Lorenzo was my last connection to Nowhere-Ville. My relationships were headed nowhere, and I was the conductor. Lorenzo made me realize that my love train was off track, and I needed to get off.

He wasn't really busted, either. He just made me see the hard-core truth, and I was not ready to hear it. Unlike Kyle and Nathan, Lorenzo was actually a good brother. Yes, girls, they are out there, but he was the right brother at the wrong time. I had so much baggage that I couldn't recognize a good man when he was staring me in the face, which I believe is the problem with women today. It's not that there aren't any good men out there; women are just so bogged down with baggage from past relationships we can't recognize a good man when we meet one. But, let me get back to Lorenzo before I get sidetracked with my soliloquies about relationships. My head was in the wrong place. I couldn't give him what he needed or wanted, which was a good woman. Hard to say, it but it's the truth.

Lorenzo was a black Puerto Rican with strong family ties and a sense of values. He was short for a man—only 5'7" or 5'8", but he was stocky and athletic. Although his background was Hispanic, you would have thought Lorenzo was straight from the Motherland. His skin was the color of night, but his hair was thick and silky. He had a smile that was magnified by a radiant personality. He was honest, responsible, compassionate, and hard working. As a federal probation officer, he had a secure job with opportunities for advancement. He and I were both twenty-six, and most of the men I knew were just getting established. Lorenzo wasn't like most of the men our age. We met at the detention center where I was working at the time.

He was there checking on a client who had been convicted for forging an exorbitant amount of money in hot checks. He asked me out, and on our first date, I realized that he was on the fast track to success; the total opposite of Nathan; therefore, I was attracted to him right away. Not only did he have his officer's salary, he also made extra money working as a security officer at night and on weekends. He had just recently bought a three-bedroom home through a home ownership program funded by the government for law enforcement officers. He was emotionally secure; he trusted me, and he wanted a woman to share his life with. He was perfect…but I wasn't.

Lorenzo had a son by his high school sweetheart. This was a major problem for me. His situation reminded me of the reason Kyle broke up with me, and Nathan's infidelity left me emotionally scarred and untrusting. I was too insecure to be in a relationship that required so much trust, yet I wanted to make something work with Lorenzo if I could.

I knew he worked all the time, but I was like Inch-high Private Eye looking for evidence to convict him with. If he worked over on a part-time, I was too quick to ask him where he had been, whom he had been with, and why was he so late. Then, his son's mother started calling all the time asking for money. Her name was Dee Dee, and I would go crazy every time she called. The mere mention of this woman's name would make me put on my clown suit and start to act a fool.

Dee Dee was a hairstylist at a beauty shop on Park Row and New York in Arlington. She must have gone to beauty school in a circus because Dee Dee created hairstyles that made women look like peacocks. You know the kind. The styles with all the gel, spritz, burgundy, gold, and royal blue highlights. And she put so much oil sheen on your hair that it looked like a grease spot on a driveway. I saw a picture of one of her clients once. The woman looked like she was auditioning for Ringling Brothers. She had a French roll in the back, Shirley Temple curls in the top, and finger waves on the side. It was all topped off by platinum blond and fuchsia highlights. *Can you believe that mess?*

Dee Dee made a good living by doing hair, but she always needed money from Lorenzo. She used their son, Antonio, as an excuse to squeeze extra cash out of him. She would call and complain that Antonio needed a new pair of $200 tennis shoes or a $100 sweat suit. If it wasn't clothes, it was furniture, "Antonio needs a new bed." If it wasn't furniture, it was food, "I'm broke, your son's hungry, and I don't have any food in the house." Lorenzo would give her five or six hundred dollars just for food. Don't get me wrong, I believe in a man taking care of his kids, but I believed that Dee Dee was using her son to get Lorenzo back. As a matter fact, I know it. She pretty much admitted as much to me when she told me one day on the phone, "I'm the mother of his child. I will always be around. All I have to do is call, and Lorenzo will be here with the quickness. Can you say the same?" I couldn't, but I didn't tell her that. I displayed my anger by being distrustful and nagging the shit out of the man.

Every time Dee Dee called, Lorenzo and I would argue then go to bed angry. I was working on my master's degree in social work, and I had a full-time job as a counselor (becoming an attorney was not an option after being on probation for a couple of years). I was financially secure and fiercely independent. I didn't need anything or anyone. I constantly reminded Lorenzo that he was privileged to be in my presence and that I didn't need him for shit. I let him know that I was not like the ghetto-girls he was used to dealing with, who had no education and no money. He eventually grew tired of me nagging him and belittling his choices in women.

"You know I'm sick and tired of feeling like a dick with a badge on it. If you don't need me, why am I here dealing with this shit?"

Flashbacks of Nathan flipping the script on me always ran through my mind when he talked to me like this. I refused to back down when I thought I was being manipulated.

"Lorenzo, if you feel used, that's on you. I don't need you for sex, either. You nor your little ass penis. My vibrator works just fine, so baby, please don't flatter yourself. I just need you to know that I'm not stupid. A man's gonna do what a man's gonna do. No matter how much you say you love me, if there's another piece of pussy out there that you want, you're gonna go and get it. There's nothing I can do to stop that, but I'll be damned if I sit here and wait on you to fool around on me. Especially, when the bitch is telling me all she has to do is call you. If you have been faithful, you eventually won't be as much as she calls you!"

"Why are you listening to that shit? You're always talking about how much you got it together and shit. If you do, why are you listening to someone you know doesn't like you? A real woman would know to trust her man and not some girl that's trying to steal him.

"That can only happen if you allow it."

"So you don't trust me?"

"I don't trust any man."

"That's not what I asked you. I'm not just any man; I'm your boyfriend. I'll ask you again. Do you trust *me*?"

I hesitated because I was hurting a good man for no reason at all. But I was in pain, too, and I didn't know what to do about it. The only thing I knew to do was lash out.

"No, I don't trust you."

He didn't lose control like I thought he would. He just shook his head and said, "Okay…It's over. You don't trust me, and you have no use for me, so I'm moving on." I was confused and hurt. I didn't think it would go this far. I thought we would argue and then have make-up sex like we always did. Lorenzo had a small penis, but he made up for with it his skills in the oral department. He at least thought about me having an orgasm; although, I hardly ever did without him going down on me. If his lips came anywhere near my pussy, I'd orgasm. I was never disappointed unless I was in the mood for the dick, and in those cases, I always had Spike, my trusty vibrator.

I didn't think Lorenzo would leave, so I decided to push him further just to see if he really meant what he said.

"Go ahead. All you're gonna do is run back to Dee Dee, so she can spend up your money! Hell, I don't need this shit. I can do bad by my damn self!"

"At least she wants me for something. You know what? I'm not doing this again. I'm not going to argue with you. I do love you, and I've never cheated on you, whether you believe it or not. Because I love you, I'm going to say this even though I know it may hurt you.

"Jaslyn, you need help. You have serious issues with men. You're going through life not trusting anybody, and it's killing you. Get help before you end up alone and bitter."

And with that he walked out the door and out of my life.

Part III
All Grown Up

Chapter 11
Barbershop

Sampson, 2001

On Saturday mornings, the fellas and I took our weekly trips to the barbershop. After graduating from college, we were managing to do very well for ourselves. Malik worked as a police officer for the Fort Worth Police Department. Jawaan taught calculus at a local high school and served as the school's head basketball coach. I was working full-time at Martin Securities in the marketing department and had just recently graduated from the M.B.A. program at Texas Christian University. Our incomes afforded us opportunities to frequent upscale, businesses but we preferred to remain in the hood when it came to maintaining our coifs. Once a black man finds a barber he can trust, he never leaves him. Never.

Saturday mornings gave us the perfect excuse for male bonding at the barbershop, which was always followed by a game of basketball that we played until we separated for our evening activities.

Womack, our barber, had been cutting our hair for years. When we were little, Jawaan's dad would take us to the shop with him on Saturdays to get our haircuts. Back then, money was tight, so Mr. Turner could only afford to take us once a month, especially since he was taking on the responsibility that belonged to two other men. As adults, we continued the custom but on a weekly basis. It was our time to catch up with each other regarding the week's events and to receive or reject sage advice from the shop's barbers and patrons.

It had been years since Layla's "Sybil" act, but I was still bewildered by my love life. I had a string of girlfriends who consistently reminded me of what it meant to have your heart broken. As always, my boys wanted the best for me and took every chance they could to discuss the situation. Malik was insistent that I join his pursuit to become Player of Year for the Dallas/Fort Worth Metroplex. He said, or did, whatever he needed to get the pussy. What he was doing couldn't even be called loving and leaving. It was more like hit-it–and–quit-it. They are not the same thing. Loving implies that he cared. He didn't, and women knew it. He did it every chance he got. Everyone knew how he was, but somehow he was still able to lure women into his web. It was probably because he had outgrown his chubby physique and bad complexion. Malik was now a strapping 6'1" tower of lean muscle. Women were constantly fawning over his smooth dark, chocolate skin and big brown eyes. He hit the gym every day, and his body showed it. Consequently, he had no problem getting women, and he wanted me to join him in doggin' the sisters out.

Jawaan, on the other hand, was the poster boy for the commitment phobic. Somehow, Tamika from junior high had managed to hold on to Jawaan. They were constantly embattled in this on-again-off-again relationship. He stood a couple of inches taller than Malik, and his skin was paper sack brown. His eyes were sharp and slanted. He kept his hair cut close in a bald fade, and he was always well-groomed. Jawaan also had no problem getting women, yet Tamika always managed to hang in there. I had to give it to him. He'd left behind his player days and actually treated Tamika like she was worthy of his respect. Jawaan never cheated on her. When he wanted to see someone else, he broke up with her, or she broke up with him when she wanted to sow her wild oats. I often wondered why they put up with each other's bullshit, but it seemed to work. Jawaan never pressured me the way Malik did, but sometimes he expressed concern for how I was dealing with my own love life.

On this particular trip to the barbershop, they both decided to address the status of my social life. We were sitting in the waiting area, which was the former living room and dining room of a converted two-bedroom home. The kitchen and bedrooms now housed the barber stations; the restroom was at the back of the house with two stalls instead of a bathtub. Except for the restroom, all the walls had been removed, and the space was open and accessible. While we were waiting to be serviced, Malik said, "You know, Sam, every time one of your girlfriends does something stupid, you go into these funky moods and don't want to be bothered. Man, you need to let that shit go and get with the program. Stop worrying about these hoes' feelings, man, and treat them the way they need to be treated. Like trash!" Right topic, wrong place.

"Can we stop discussing my business in the middle of this shop? All of Stop Six can hear you!" I tried to divert attention from me, but it was too late. The shop lit up with opinions from every brother waiting for his turn at being the male Oprah Winfrey. Womack started talking first.

"What? Sam got woman problems?"

"No, I don't; thank you very much."

"Mack, he's lying. These girls have got him coming and going!" Jawaan had to add his two cents into the mix.

"Well, what's the problem, young blood?" Womack was talking to me, but Malik answered.

"This crazy fool keeps falling in love. Trying to find the perfect woman and shit. I keep telling him that HIV killed love like crack killed pimpin'!"

"Negro, shut up! That shit don't make no sense," Jawaan was back at it now and capitalizing on the opportunity to prove to Malik that he was ignorant, while everyone in the shop laughed.

"Whatever, punk! It's the truth."

"Boy, what do you know about pimpin'?" Chicago, a barber who took his moniker from his city of birth and our resident hustling authority, decided to offer his expertise. Chicago was about twenty-seven or twenty-eight years old. At 5'7" tall, he was the flyest barber I had ever seen. He often cut hair in silk shirts, slacks, and alligator shoes (how his feet never hurt was beyond me). He wore his hair in cornrows with a baby hair edge-up that made him look like the R&B singer, Ginuwine. In his younger days, Chicago hustled women, weed, crack, stolen cars, TVs, and radios. Hell, he even hustled bootlegged videos and CDs. After two trips to the Illinois Department of Corrections, he moved to Texas and was now hustling haircuts. As in all his hustles, he was very successful. He could have had his own shop had he not had a habit of taking off for every holiday. His birthday, July 4th, Labor Day, Columbus Day, Ground Hog's Day, you name it. He even took off for Juneteenth, which was a Texas holiday, but since he had been here for a while, he celebrated it just as eagerly as we did. Chicago still had the hustler's lifestyle in his blood, though, which required the least amount of work while making the maximum amount of income. He knew Malik had no idea what he was talking about, and he couldn't resist imparting us with his knowledge of the pimp game, while at the same time, correcting Malik, whom he hated, because he was a member of the very people that ran him out his hometown six years ago— the police.

"Malik don't know what the hell he's talking about, Sam, but he does have a point. You can't be out there with your nose wide open. You have to remember. Women are not to be trusted. Not one of 'em! Hell, I don't even trust my own mama. Why? Because she's a woman. Anybody that bleeds for a whole week out of the month and still lives cannot be trusted."

We all yelled out, "Ugh! You are *so* nasty!"

"It's the truth. You can't trust women because they don't know what the hell they want. One minute, they want a brother who's sensitive and compassionate. A trick who'll take care of they asses. You know, a man with benefits. When they get him, they treat him like shit because he's too nice. The next minute, they want a rough neck. A man with a spine. Somebody who'll stand up to them. The next thing you know, they complainin' and shit talkin' 'bout how the brotha's abusin' 'em and shit. Women don't know what they want so you have to know for 'em. And if anybody's gonna give it to 'em, it might as well be you. And another thing, always remember that a woman will do anything whether they say they will or not. They're just looking for the right man to persuade them to do it. You know those chicks—the ones who are always yelling I was tipsy; I didn't know what I was doing."

"You must be out of your damn mind," Womack admonished. "Sam, don't listen to that cat. You'll end up in jail!"

Chicago wasn't finished, though. "Just remember, Sam, get them before they get you."

"It's not that bad, fellas. Believe me." I was to be ignored as every man in the shop became an expert on my love life. I squirmed in my seat as Reuben, a truck driver in his late forties, decided to add his opinion, while the two that started it all sat back giggling like two elves in Santa's workshop.

"He's a little over the top, but Chicago is right about one thing. Don't be out there waiting for a woman to break your heart. I fell in love once, in my twenty's. I asked the girl to marry me. All she said was 'Uh huh', then she put the ring on the coffee table and started watching *All in the Family* like ain't shit happened. I later found out that she was sleeping with my cousin. That's really fucked up!"

"It sure is Reuben. Listen up, Sam," Womack's turn had come back around, and I knew I was in for it. Jawaan and Malik were really laughing now because they knew what they had started. Once Womack was on a roll, he was impossible to stop.

"You can only be good to a woman for so long. Once you start being good to them they, start nagging your ass until you're like that game at the State Fair where they hit you over the head with a hammer, and you pop your top. Once a woman starts nagging you, you just explode."

I asked, "But you've been married for over 30 years; how can you buy into what these assholes are saying?"

"Don't get me wrong, Sam. I love my wife. I care for her deeply, and I come from a time where a man did not leave his family no matter how bad it got. But that woman has pushed me to my limits, and I'm sure that I have pushed her to hers. But, because we believed in something deeper and higher than ourselves, we had a chance to make it through. You young people don't have no faith. You want everything quick–right now. Faith is not a quick thing. You have to wait on Jesus, and he'll make things happen in his own time and that includes falling in love." *Now why do old people always have to bring up Jesus?* Here I am sharing my business with all of Fort Worth, and he wants to get all holier-than-thou on me. Evidently, he hadn't read the exasperated expression on my face because he kept going. "If I had a chance to do it all over again, I would not try to fall in love so fast. I'd get to know myself, first. If you don't know and love yourself, you won't be any good to anyone else. There's nothing wrong with love, just make sure that you are not trying to fill that empty space inside you with someone else's dreams and aspirations. 'Cause what you're lookin' for, you can't find in any woman. Hell, you can't find it in any person. You can only find it in the Lord. Look deeper than yourself."

Malik had had all that he could stand. Always the clown, he yells out, "Grasshopper, snatch the pebble from my hand." We all laughed as the conversation turned to the President and his so-called tax breaks.

I was hearing Womack, but I wasn't listening. I was young and still quite immature. I wasn't ready for the truth, so I chose to live somewhere between Malik, the player, and Jawaan, the serial monogamist. I played the field with a twist. I told the truth. I just wanted to have sex–no strings attached.

Chapter 13
Revelations

Sampson, 2003

To a complete stranger, I was the picture of perfection. On the surface, I was a polished, successful black man. After Layla, I managed to graduate from college with a degree in marketing, and when I received my M.B.A., I started an advertising agency. My company, Tate & Associates, had a lucrative contract with a major soft drink company, which gave me the exclusive advertising rights to its southwest region. I was living quite comfortably. To treat myself for all my dedication and hard work, I allowed myself a few extravagances. I bought a luxury condo in Las Colinas and had graduated from the Ford Ranger to a fully-loaded, black Range Rover with the leather interior. Okay, okay, I am bragging but shit, I deserved it, and I'm proud of what I have accomplished. I was the veritable bootstraps man. I wouldn't necessarily align myself with the philosophies of Clarence Thomas, but I had managed to overcome difficult odds through self-discipline, education, and determination.

I haven't been able to get Aunt Tootie out of the ghetto, though. It's not because I can't afford it but because she doesn't want to leave. She likes staying in Stop Six. All of her friends are there, and her church is there. Furthermore, Uncle Junior is there, so she definitely ain't going nowhere. I do look after her, however, making sure that she needs and wants for nothing.

My professional life made the average brother green with envy. My social life, however, was another matter. Underneath all the trappings of my success, I was a mess. In the past, I allowed women to get close to me and then use that closeness to exploit me. I couldn't take it anymore. My heart now had a "no trespassing" sign on it to be sure that no one got close to it.

I developed a series of girlfriends whose sole purpose was to satisfy me sexually. Chicago's advice stayed with me.

"I'll get them before they get me" was my new motto. Many women approached me for sex, and every time I left a woman's bed in the middle of the night and every time I would pull a woman close to me emotionally and then shut her out by becoming aloof, was revenge for the way I had been treated. I never lied to anyone about what I was looking for. They needed to know from day one that love didn't live here, anymore. The game plan—*only fuck buddies need apply*—and believe it or not, it worked. One girl just flat out told me, "I just want to fuck," and I was happy to oblige. Most women went along with the program just to see if they could change me. They had the game so twisted. One young lady was particularly bitter with the outcome of our relationship. Her name was Catina Sanders, and we used to work together before I started my company. We were both rookies in the marketing department at the securities firm I worked for, and we struck up a friendship because we were the new kids on the block. One day after work, I invited Catina out for drinks. We went to shoot pool and to have a few beers. The girl couldn't handle her liquor and got a little too friendly. I escorted her home to make sure that she made it safely. As I was about to leave, she invited me into her apartment.

"You're drunk, and I don't want to take advantage of you. Besides, I'm not looking to date anyone. We work together, and if things don't work out, that could make us both uncomfortable."

"I'm not that drunk. I know what I want, and what I want is you. I'm a big girl, and I can handle myself."

Who was I to deny a girl that knew what she wanted. Hell, I wanted it too. Catina and I slept with each other off and on for several months, but soon, her attitude started to change. She started calling me *just because,* and she wanted to take walks in the park *just to talk.* Eventually, she started sending me little notes and small gift baskets to show me how she felt. I didn't know what to do, so I did the only thing I knew how to do and that was to push her away. If she called, I didn't return her calls. When she wanted to hang out, I was always busy. After we had sex, I made it a point to leave her house, immediately, and I never invited her over to my place. One day, she asked me about it.

"When are you going to invite me over to your house?"

"For what?"

"What do you mean for what? We've been kicking it for almost a year now, and I still don't know where you live."

"I don't see why it's necessary for you to know where I live. We are just kicking it, right?"

"Yeah, but still…"

"But what? I'm not trying to hurt your feelings, but if we're going to continue seeing each other, then things have to remain simple. We don't want to complicate the situation by becoming too involved in each other's lives. So, let's just keep things like they are."

"What if I think the situation should change?"

"Then I think things are over."

"What? How can you throw this relationship away so easily?

"What relationship? We fuck. That's it. Don't get it twisted. I told you the deal when we started seeing each other. If you thought it was turning into something else, then that's your fault. Not mine."

She was livid. "Get out. Right now. Just leave my house and don't ever come back!"

I was cool with the way things ended. That is until Catina was promoted over me. You know how it goes. No report was ever good enough. I had to do all my research over because it had to be just right. My evaluations were becoming extremely unsatisfactory. I quit before she got the chance to fire me. I should have filed sexual harassment charges against her, but I wanted to do my own thing, anyway. I had just received my graduate degree and had learned everything I could from that company, so I took that opportunity to start my agency.

I didn't want to change, but I didn't want to hurt women, either. I didn't want to feel anything, so I continued to believe that I was satisfied with what I had become. But as more women fell in love with me only to find that I was unavailable, emotionally, the more hearts I broke. I couldn't do anything about it. Didn't want to. For the next two years, I grew into a thirty-two year-old man whose only purpose in life was tricking his dick off.

My fear of vulnerability lead to an emotional emptiness that I knew needed to be filled. I took time off from women, period. No more fuck buddies for me. Three things precipitated that change: my brother Solomon became a minister; Jawaan became engaged, and Malik went to jail.

Solomon was always a spiritual individual. When we were young, he chose to get baptized at the age of twelve; whereas, I was almost eighteen. Solomon always wanted to go to church, but I felt like I was being forced to go as punishment for some unknown crime I didn't know that I had committed. He always sang in the choir, served on the usher board, and participated in all the activities for the youth department. In college, he joined the gospel choir on campus, and he even started a bible study group in his dormitory. Every decision he made was always grounded in spirituality, but his decision to be a minister was still a shock.

One Saturday afternoon, he came to my condo to visit me.

"Yo, Sam, what's up?"

"Nothing. How you been?" We hugged, as only black men know how, like we were performing some secret handshake to which no one else could know the sequence. We sat down in the living room to watch *Sportscenter* on ESPN.

"I'm doing alright. I stopped by today to share some news with you."

"What? You're not getting married are you? Please tell me it's not that buck-toothed broad in the choir!" The women at church, even the old ones, were always after Solomon. Except for his deep bronze complexion, we were spitting images of each other. We always assumed we had the same father, but we were never certain.

He laughed and said, "Lucretia is her name. Now you know you are wrong for that. There is nothing wrong with Sister Miles."

"Whatever." I shook my head and took a sip of my beer.

"I'm not getting married, but I am making a commitment. A commitment to God…I'm going to be a minister."

"What the hell?" I almost choked.

"I just wanted you to be the first to know, that's all."

"Well, I'm happy for you man, if that's what you want. I kind of felt like that's where you were headed, anyway. That's a big responsibility. Are you sure this is what you want to do?"

"I'm sure. I've known for years and avoided it. I can't run from it any longer."

"Have you told Aunt Tootie and Uncle Junior?

"No, not yet. I want you to be there when I do.'

"No problem, man. Aunt Tootie will love it…Uncle Junior will probably have a hear attack!" We both laughed and began discussing the Mavericks and their success as a basketball team.

The next day after church, Solomon shared his good news with Aunt Tootie and Uncle Junior. As we predicted, she was elated. Junior didn't have a heart attack, but he did get drunk as hell. That was always his response to everything, so I wasn't shocked that night when my aunt called to say that Junior had been arrested for public drunkenness. He had fallen asleep in front of the corner store and had urinated on himself when a police patrol car pulled into the parking lot. He was taken to the station to sleep it off. Typical!

A week had passed since Solomon revealed his plans to become a minister. I told Solomon that I was cool with his decision, but it really bothered me and I wanted to talk to someone about it. I made a point to meet with Jawaan Friday after work to drink a few beers, watch the Mavericks, and discuss my concerns about my brother.

We went to a sports bar in Deep Ellum to chill out after work and relax. Deep Ellum was located in Dallas, and even though we lived practically thirty minutes away, we often liked to hang out there because it was close to where we worked. My office was located in downtown Dallas, and Jawaan's high school was in South Dallas. Since we were both only 10 minutes away from Deep Ellum, it was the perfect location. The fact that it was a black-owned establishment was an added bonus.

It was Tuesday evening, and this particular bar broadcasted all the Mavericks games and served a banging Cajun buffet. I was looking forward to getting my grub on and unloading my burdens. As we sat down in a corner booth with our plates full of fried catfish, jambalaya, gumbo, and dirty rice, I initiated a discussion of Solomon's career decision.

"Did Solomon tell you that he's decided to become a minister?"

"Really? No, he didn't tell me. Man, that's great news!"

"Yeah, it is, isn't it," I replied forlornly.

"You sound upset. Why?"

"I don't know. It's like I'm losing my little brother."

"You're not losing him, fool. He's just growing up and finding his place in the world. Something you need to do."

"What?" I was definitely perplexed, if not pissed. Here I was trying to unload my feelings about my brother, and my best friend was trying to turn the tables on me.

"Look, Sam, I love you like a play cousin…"

"FUUUCCK YOUUU!" We laughed knowing that he was just as much a brother to me as Solomon was.

"Like I was saying, I care about you, and I try my best to stay out of your business, unless you ask me to, you know? But, I've watched you for years trying to bury yourself in these relationships that don't mean anything. Either you are totally whipped or you go around like Jiffy Dick trying to service every woman you meet with a piece of tail. You need to face reality and understand that the world is moving on without you. You've got lots of material things, but you're not fulfilled. You've got a nice crib, a fly ass car and all that, but it's not making you happy.

"You're not upset with Solomon because you're losing him. You're upset because he's happy. He's satisfied with the life he's chosen, and you're not, so you don't understand what he's doing. Stop being afraid, man. Open yourself up so that you can be satisfied with women and life. It all goes together. Don't you see?"

Now, I was really pissed. Jawaan was dead on, but denial is a hard habit to break. "No, I don't see. How the fuck do you know what makes me happy?" I could feel the veins in my forehead about to burst. "This was not about me. Not at all. And I don't appreciate you throwing my sex life up in my face like that. Who says I'm not satisfied? You? Who are you to talk about being fulfilled when you been fuckin' the same woman for the last fifteen years and won't commit to her? Who else am I supposed to pattern my happiness after? Malik? The misogynist who hates his damn mama so much that every woman he encounters has to suffer for it? It seems like I'm lacking in role models when it comes to opening my heart! And aren't you the same mothafuckas who told me never to trust a woman? So, just why the fuck should I put myself in the precarious position of falling in love? Huh?!"

My voice had risen above the five televisions broadcasting the Mavericks game, above the sound of music pulsating from the juke box, above the buzz and banter of people conversing about the week's end. It seemed that all eyes were focused on me and my table. All the noise had come to an abrupt halt waiting for the conflict that was certain to follow.

Jawaan remained silent. The patrons returned to their conversations as I sat waiting for Jawaan to respond. I was shocked when I looked in his eyes, and I didn't see anger. Jawaan's eyes were full of disappointment. I looked down at my drink. I was ashamed of my behavior, and I didn't know how to make it right. Tension permeated the air between us. "I'm sorry," was my feeble attempt to break the silence. For a few moments, he maintained his silence, but then, he finally spoke to me. Without yelling or screaming, but with a clipped and measured intensity that belied how he was really feeling.

"Nigga, you must be crazy. Fuck that sorry ass apology. I love you, and everything, but you must be smoking crack if you think I'm about to let you sit here and talk to me like that.

Shit, you've got life all fucked up. I'm trying to help you. I see your pain everyday. Every time you make a date and come back from one, I don't see happiness or sadness. Shit, I don't even see shame in you. You wanna know what I see, Sampson? Do you?" Jawaan was always my rock, and I had pushed him to his limits. He had not called me Sampson since the first day we met as kids at Dunbar. His words were coming at me all at once but still he had not raised his voice. The disappointment was still evident on his face, and it was focused on getting me to see his point. With crinkled eyebrows and eyes focused, I knew he was concentrating on what he saying.

With uncertainty in my voice, I confessed, "Yeah, man, I do. What do you see?"

"I see disgust. You're disgusted with yourself and who you've become. Who am I to ask you about your sex life or to know what makes you happy? I'm your best fucking friend, and I've known you most of your life. You've known me most of mine. I was there when Alicia dumped your ass at the prom, and I was there when Asia burnt your measly dick, *and* I was there when Layla tried to kill herself. And so was Solomon. And so was Malik. So I don't want to hear shit about you not having anyone to turn to. Oh, and that girl I've been fucking off-and-on for the last fifteen years without a commitment…we're getting married. So it looks to me, Sampson, that you're the only one who's afraid of putting yourself out there." He stopped just before he started raising his voice. His breathing was hard and fast. I knew he was getting angry, but somewhere inside him, Jawaan found the compassion and strength to turn the conversation around.

"Man, I hate to see you like this. You're a stand-up guy. You've got a lot to offer, but whether you want to believe it or not, you're bitter, and it's destroying you."

Someone stole my voice because I had no words. Even if I had, they would not have been enough to convey what I was feeling. Looking at your life through the mirror of your friend's assessment can cause insurmountable pain. My feelings were lying wide open on the beach of hostility and despair, and I was waiting for the monsoon to come along and wash away the pain. Why did I care? Why did I bother with the emotional baggage of falling in love? I had everything I needed. My career was booming, and here I was despairing about not having someone to love me. *Who gives a shit?* I did.

I gulped down my beer instead of trying to talk. Jawaan was not letting me off that easy. Again, he took the reigns of the conversation.

"Sam, it would be different if you *were* more like Malik, and you didn't care about anybody, but you're not. You're just not like that, man, so stop trying to be someone you're not. Period.

"In all the other areas, of your life you learn as much as you can about a situation, and then, you explore all your options. You never close yourself off to opportunities. Why aren't you the same way with relationships?"

I was still drinking my beer, staring off at the television pretending to be aloof and unaffected. The waitress provided me with a much-needed escape.

"Another round, gentleman?" came a voice from a woman with blond hair who appeared to be barely above the legal drinking age herself. All I could think about was how ironic it was for this young white girl to be working in a black owned sports bar. *Making money is universal,* I laughed to myself.

"Sure," I said.

She refilled our mugs with beer and set the pitcher in the middle of the table for our convenience and walked away.

"Anyway, just think about what I'm saying, man."

"Sure." It seemed to be the only word I knew at the moment.

"Okay, change of subject. Don't you wanna know more about my engagement?" Just like that I was out of the hot seat.

"Hell, no! You're marrying that ghetto-ass Tamika. Shit, she'll probably have you getting married in her granny's backyard with Kentucky Fried Chicken as the caterer and red Kool-Aid for champagne."

"Damn right! And for entertainment, we gon' bust out the spades and dominoes tables. Ain't no other way to do it!

Anyway, you're just mad because I pulled your hoe card." We both laughed. We finished consuming our beers and food. Just like that, things were back to normal.

Chapter 14
The Pussy Addiction

Over the past few months, Solomon and Jawaan had given me a lot to think about. I knew my love life needed to be revamped, but I wasn't quite ready to change. It seems sometimes that events happen one right after the other to make you re-evaluate your life's goals. After these events take place, you either fold under the pressure, or you take stock of who you are and where your life is going. Then, you decide to change your plans in order to survive. The final factor that preceded my social restructuring began one night at four in the morning. I was in the middle of a dream about Halle Berry when my phone rang. We were in a hot tub in Mexico drinking margaritas and were just about to get our freak on when the shrill of the phone's bell brought me out of my fantasy. I was pissed.

"Who the hell is this?" I barked.

"This is the Southwestern Bell telephone operator. Would you like to accept a collect phone call from Malik Wallace?"

I was groggy from sleeping, and I thought I was still dreaming. I was confused and not quite clear on what I had just heard; it was taking me a minute to get my thoughts together.

"Sir, would you like to accept a collect call from Malik Wallace?"

Then, I heard Malik's voice in the background. "Accept the call, fool!"

"What…oh, yeah…I'll accept."

"Thank you," the operator proclaimed politely and left us to our call. By this time, I had gathered my wits. I was anxious to see what was so urgent that it couldn't wait until daybreak and why in the world he was calling me collect.

"Man, I need you to come and get me out of jail."

"What?!" I was wide-awake now.

"I'm in jail. I need you to bail me out."

"What the fuck happened? Why the hell are you in jail?"

"Just come get me. I'll tell you when you get here. I'm in a holding tank right now, but they can only keep me in here for so long. Once, I'm placed in the regular tank, you know my ass is toast. You know they hate cops in jail. They'll put me protective custody, but if these fools have a chance to get me, then I'll get my ass beat. Now hurry the fuck up!"

I heard the urgency in his voice and knew this was no joke. As I hopped out of bed, I started changing into my clothes from the night before, which were on the bench at the foot of my bed. Fortunately, I had been too exhausted to put them in the hamper.

"How much is your bail?"

"Five hundred. There's a bondsmen who will be waiting on you at the front of the jail to speed up the process. He's a friend of mine so give him the money, and I'll get out faster. Just hurry up, okay!"

"Well, what jail are you in?"

"Tarrant County. Now, please hurry, Sam."

He sounded like he was about to cry. "Okay, okay. I'm on my way. Oh, Malik."

"Yeah?"

"Don't drop the soap!" I laughed. I couldn't resist getting in a quick dig. He lost it.

"Fuck you, man! Fuck you! Just come and get me!"

He hung up the phone. After I stopped laughing, I called Jawaan. *Shit, shit, shit! What the hell is Malik doing in jail?* Before I could let my thoughts wander any further, Tamika answered the phone.

"Tamika, it's Sam. Let me talk to Jawaan."

"Sampson, why are you calling my house so early in the damn morning? Don't you know that folks are sleeping?

"First of all, it's not your house, yet. Right now, you're just a houseguest. Second, this is an emergency, so could you please put Jawaan on the phone? I seriously don't have time for games."

"Whatever! Hold on." I heard her waking him in the background. "Baby, it's Sam. He says it's important."

Jawaan took the phone and whispered, "Yeah, man. What up?"

"Malik's in jail and wants us to bail him out. Meet me at Tarrant County jail in fifteen minutes."

"I'm on my way, man, but I'm broke. I just spent my last few dollars on the wedding."

"Don't sweat it, man. I have the money."

"Alright, I'm on my way."

We hung up the phone. I finished dressing and jumped in the car. I prayed that I didn't end up going to jail for speeding because Las Colinas was at least twenty minutes away from downtown Fort Worth, but I drove my truck like I was on an autobahn freeway trying to help a friend in need. Plus, my curiosity was killing me. I wanted to know how a decorated police officer could end up in jail.

When I arrived, Jawaan was already there and had somehow managed to meet the bondsman. They had just met and were about to get into the details of the case when I walked in. I gave the bondsman the money, and he left to go make Malik's bail.

"Did he say why Malik is in jail?"

"No, he was about to tell me when you showed up. I guess Malik is so pressed to get out he wanted to take care of that first."

"Oh."

We sat down and waited for Malik's release. Two hours passed before they finally let him go. When he came out he was still in his officer's uniform, which was wrinkled and unbuttoned at the collar.

He collected his items from the intake officer and walked over to where Jawaan and I were seated.

"Thanks, dogs. I owe you. Big Time."

"What happened?" I asked

"Can we get something to eat? I've been in this jail all night, and I'm starving."

Malik rode in the car with me since his had been impounded. Jawaan followed closely behind. We drove to International House of Pancakes on University Drive near downtown. I chose it partly because it was close and partly because I didn't want anyone we knew to see us. I wasn't embarrassed. I just wanted to hear this story without any interruptions.

We entered the restaurant and were immediately seated by our hostess. The waitress came, and we placed our orders for breakfast; then Jawaan and I sat silently and waited for an explanation.

"I got arrested."

Jawaan and I both stared backed with expressions as if to say "Duh!"

"For solicitation."

"What were you soliciting?" Jawaan was definitely dumbfounded. He almost sounded like a kid on Sesame Street. *It couldn't be what we were both thinking.*

"Sex," he said casually.

"What the hell?" I was flabbergasted. "Man, you can have any woman you want. Why in the hell would you try to pay for pussy?"

"Listen to the whole story first, okay?"

"We're waiting," I demanded.

"When I got off work, I was a little horny. You know...I just wanted to look at some tits and ass without any strings, so I went over to Sweet Charlie's, this strip joint on the north side. Off of 28th Street."

"No need to tell me where it is, "I commented snidely.

"That's because you already know where it is!"

"Stop playin' and just finish the damn story."

"Well, I wasn't going to stay long. That's why I didn't think to take off my uniform. When I got there, I had a few drinks, and I went to the stage. There was this dancer...she was slammin'! Man, she was brick-house fine. Plus, she was the only black chick in the joint. All the other dancers were Hispanic or white. She got to shaking her ass all in my face, and I couldn't help myself! Before I knew it, I had grabbed her by the butt and was trying to put her on my lap. But this bouncer showed up and grabbed me by the shoulder and tells me in no uncertain terms, 'NO TOUCHING.' Dude looked like Stone Cold Steve Austin from the WWF, so I wasn't arguing. I let the girl go, and she got back on stage to finish dancing. But then, the bouncer whispers in my ear that if I wanted some serious action I could go to this room in the back, and old girl would meet me in there.

"To make a long story short, I go to the room, and ten minutes later, Brick House shows up. We don't even talk, she just sticks her tongue down my throat. Then, all of sudden she breaks away from me and starts massaging my dick through my pants. My dick is ROCK HARD when she finally tells me that we can do whatever I want for fifty bucks. So, I'm like 'Whatever? Even head?' She says, 'Yeah.' So, I pull out the money, give it to her, and say 'Let's do this.' She must have had a wire in her g-string because the next thing I know, in walks Stone Cold yelling, 'You're under arrest.' He put the handcuffs on me, and presto, here I am.

"Can you believe this broad was an undercover cop? Turns out they were conducting some type of sting operation, and everyone who got busted that night will be included in a cover story for the *Star-Telegram*."

Speechless was an understatement. While Malik was talking, our food arrived. I stared at my best friend with my mouth agape, but Jawaan must have been falling in love with his eggs and pancakes because he couldn't, or wouldn't, look up. Malik, however, was tearing into his steak and eggs.

Somewhere, I found the nerve to say, "You mean to tell me you're about to lose your damn job because your dumb ass got busted at a strip joint in uniform trying to buy some trim?! How stupid can you be? Do you have "idiot" stamped across your birth certificate or what? Man, you're not that fat kid anymore. You don't have to struggle to get girls. Why on earth would you do something that stupid?"

Between mouthfuls of steak, he said, "What can I say, man? I have a pussy addiction."

"A pussy addiction? What the hell is that?"

"You know…I'm like the girl in Spike Lee's movie. I gotta have it. No matter what. If you put it in my face, I'm going for it. It has nothing to do with relationships. It's just pussy."

"Nigga, please! You don't have a damn pussy addiction. You've got a problem alright, but it ain't pussy. You need help. To put your job at risk like that…Man, you've hated women since your Dad left, and you watched your Mom do some crazy shit to keep you guys together. You seriously need to deal with that shit, and your attitude towards women, before you go back to jail." I thought Malik would get upset with me, but I didn't care. Jawaan had kept it real with me, so it was my turn to keep it real with Malik, especially since Jawaan still had nothing to say. Unlike me, however, Malik was unfazed. He was acting like this was a normal everyday occurrence for him.

"Sam, I'm not worried about my job. I'll find another one. What did that comedian say? 'I was looking for a job when I found this one.' As far as my mother, that's none of your business. Don't talk about her like that. Ever. Or I'll kick your ass. You hear me? Furthermore, I don't need help…I need pussy. I like trim, and trim likes me, and I'll do whatever I can to get it." And with that, he was through talking. He finished his breakfast; I took him home, and Jawaan went home to Tamika.

I did some serious thinking that day. I started wondering, were the absence of my mother and the lack of a strong female figure in my life the reasons for my problems with women. Aunt Tootie was great, but when it came to pleasing Uncle Junior, that always came first. I remember always feeling left out and empty in those situations. It's the same feeling I get now in my relationships–like I'm missing something.

I loved Malik, but I didn't want to end up like him. Unable to cope with my feelings, so I had to find illegal, illicit, or immoral ways to feel better about myself. Pussy wasn't the only sedative men used to numb the pain. Alcohol also did the trick. I watched Uncle Junior use alcohol as a sedative all my life, and I saw what it did to him. He was an abusive, pissy, drunk, who couldn't take care of himself. Drugs also did the trick. Before my mom left, she was using cocaine as her sedative. It had her so bad she abandoned her family.

I could follow their paths or face the truth and deal with the pain. I chose the latter. With Malik's arrest, Solomon's news, and all Jawaan and I had discussed about my relationships, I knew it was time for a change.

Chapter 15
B.A.N's

Jaslyn, March 2003

When Lorenzo left, I thought I would hit rock bottom. Quite the contrary. I held my shit together. I kept everything on the inside. I was not about to allow these trifling men to see that they could get the best of me. No, absolutely not! And, I was not about to sit around twiddling my thumbs waiting for one of them to marry me, either. Instead, I decided to beat them at their own game. Why should I tie myself down when they weren't trying to do it?

I decided that the best plan of action for infidelity was to beat it at the pass. There couldn't be any misunderstandings about faithfulness if my partner was already in a committed relationship to someone else. The perfect man for me, I deduced, was a married man. Vincent, my lover, provided the best all-around sexual experience I'd ever had. He was willing to try, and do, anything. With him, I was a totally uninhibited nymphomaniac, or at least as close to one as I'd ever become. He would often tell me that he liked me because I liked to try new things, and his wife was a prude. This he said while he was handcuffed to the bed. What he didn't realize was that I didn't care whether or not he liked me. I don't even remember how I met him. All I remember is that when I did meet him I knew, immediately, that I wanted to fuck him. I was only involved with him because he was convenient. I didn't have to worry about whether or not he was being faithful. That was his wife's problem. I didn't have to worry about where he was going when he left my bed. That, too, was a problem for a wife to be concerned with. I was free to do whatever I wanted, whenever I wanted. The way I looked at it, I had all the benefits of a relationship without all of the complications. I could lie and say that Vincent lied to me in the beginning about his status, but I won't. I knew from the very beginning he was married. I didn't care. I couldn't allow myself to care because if I did, I was in jeopardy of losing control and falling in love—and that was out of the question!

But, why is it that when you are proactively single, people want to convince you there's something wrong with your lifestyle? Here I was taking charge of my life, and my friends and family thought something was wrong with me. It didn't matter that I was a successful therapist and was planning to one day open a group home for battered women. It didn't matter that I was in great shape because I rode my bike three miles every day, and I did crunches until I virtually had abs of steel. It didn't matter that I received numerous civic awards from community organizations for starting a mentoring program for at-risk youth. No, none of that mattered to my family and friends. All that mattered to them was that I didn't have a man of my own in my life.

After going to jail, I had turned my life from tragedy to triumph. I was aggressively pursuing my career, and men were only going to slow me down. People were constantly trying to convince me that I needed to settle down. On my 30th birthday, my family threw me a party and held, I guess, what they might call a relationship intervention.

It was a small party, but I was looking forward to it, nonetheless. Only my sisters, my mom, Shelly, and Lisa were there, but we celebrated with the obligatory cake and ice cream, which is why I like to refer to this gathering as a party. Actually, we met at one of my favorite Italian restaurants for Sunday brunch, and they brought the cake and ice cream. We'd been eating for about an hour and were laughing, talking and enjoying each other's company when out of the blue, my sister Francine asked me, "Girl, you're getting old, and your eggs are drying up. When are you going to stop running the streets and settle down?"

I knew they had been talking when everyone at the table started agreeing and shaking their heads. Francine had a knack for cutting to the chase and saying what everyone else was thinking. Most of the time, I appreciated her candor, but since it was now directed at me, and my sex life, I was not feeling Francine's bluntness.

"I thought this was a celebration, not an interrogation!"

Carol decided it was time to add a bit of tact to the intervention by saying, "Look, Jazz, we know you've been hurt, but you have to bounce back and truly move on. I know you think you are satisfied with the relationship you have with Vincent, but you're not being honest with yourself. You want more than that. Shit, you deserve more than that! You're not risking anything by sleeping with someone who doesn't have to make a commitment to you. Actually, you're risking more than his wife. You'll end up losing your self-respect, and you can't put a price on that. You know you've truly moved on when you can risk your heart again, *with* someone who can love you in return." Carol had grown into a woman who was in touch with her feelings and tried to help everyone else get in touch with theirs.

Of all the people in the world, I loved and respected my sisters and my two best friends the most. They were all beautiful and successful. Carol had the perfect nuclear family. She was a pharmacist with a husband, three kids—two boys and a girl ages fifteen, eleven, and nine—and a home in Tanglewood, an affluent neighborhood on the southwest side of town near TCU. The embodiment of the soccer mom, her hair was thick and full of body, and she was always impeccably dressed. Francine was a little jazzier. She wasn't married, but she was in a committed relationship with Morris, her boyfriend of eight years. They lived in an apartment on the west side of town, and for the most part, they got along great. They were what we called "common-law." They had lived together for so long they were practically married, and they could divide up their assets legally. So, when Morris did act up, he quickly got it together knowing she was going to take him for all he was worth, which wasn't much. In fact, Francine had decided to solidify their relationship even further because she was four months pregnant with their first child. When she wasn't taking care of Morris, Francine was a registered nurse for the county hospital. Melissa had even more spunk than Francine. She wore her hair in a short pixie cut that exemplified her sassy personality. Melissa was the type of woman that would never grow old. Her attitude said that she looked good and always would. Damon's hustle (I'm not sure exactly what his hustle was, and I never asked; I think it was bootlegging CDs) was a bit lucrative; therefore, Melissa didn't have to work. All she did was take care of the twins who were now six years old. We were all around the same mahogany skin tone, and we all inherited the Davenport almond-shaped eyes and high cheekbones.

Shelly and Lisa were also coming along in life. Although we all chose different career paths, we had managed to stay friends. As a matter of fact, they were the ones I called to bail me out of jail the night I caught Nathan with Snow White. My family still doesn't know about the arrest, and if I can help it, they never will. They think that I broke up with Nathan because he wouldn't get a job, which is partly the truth, and that I decided to become a therapist to help abused women, which is also partly the truth. Shellie was now a manager at a major department store, and she thoroughly enjoyed the twenty percent discount on designer clothes (and so did I), so she was always well dressed. She and I were about the same color and were often mistaken for sisters. Although still slender, Lisa could no longer be mistaken for a boy. She was an attractive, intelligent woman. She worked as a producer on an all-news radio station, but she was trying to get a position at the newest hip-hop station with the sole purpose of meeting her favorite artist…DJ Quik!

They had all been there for me during the toughest times in my life, and I valued their opinions, tremendously. Needless to say, I was a bit dismayed when they started attacking my social life. I immediately became defensive.

"Will you all leave me the f…," I looked at my mother who was staring at me from across the table and giving me that *You'd better not* look, and I decided to slow my roll. "Look, just leave me alone, okay? I refuse to be like the women at my shelter, so severely in need of love they are willing to become involved in abusive relationships to get it. I am very satisfied with my love life. If I don't have a problem with it, why should you? I came here to celebrate. Not talk about men."

Melissa answered my request with, "We're just trying to help. The way you're living your life can't be fulfilling. Especially to you. You're always considering other peoples' opinions and shit. And you've never been one to settle for anything, then why settle for another woman's husband? You need to stop fooling with these *bans* and get with a real man!"

The girl had just confused me. Here we were talking about men and now she was talking about deodorant. What was the deal?

"What's a ban?" I asked.

"A Bullshit Ass Nigga. You know the type of brother who only wants you for one thing. He won't get up and get a job, so you have to take care of his ass. A BAN is a man that will lie, play around, or who always has excuses about why he can't do shit. He can't do shit for you but always wants you to do something for him. And he'll cheat on his wife and lie to his girlfriend about the fact that his wife doesn't understand him and that's why he's cheating. Sound familiar? The only thing they care about is what's between your legs…Well, I better stop 'cause I forgot mama was here."

"You don't have to stop on my account. I've had my share of bans, so I know exactly what you're talking about?"

"You do?" we all asked incredulously.

"Of course! I went through my share of sorry men before I met your father." Leonard and Virginia Davenport were divorced when I was five. My mother never said a negative word about him. I didn't understand why the relationship didn't work, and I never asked. My father eventually remarried and moved to Oklahoma. He often called us and sent us money for school, but that's as close as we ever became to him. My mother rarely talked about him, and she never talked to us about her sex life or ours. All she ever told us was that there was nothing open after midnight but legs and Seven-Elevens, so it was surprising to see her join in our conversation. She was sitting at the head of the table enjoying a cigarette and a cup of coffee when she decided to impart us with her knowledge.

"I remember I was dating this guy named Walter. It was the summer of '56, and I was about to be a senior in high school. We had been seeing each other for a while. One night, we were at a party, and I found out he had been dating one of my good friends. Her name was Betty, and Walter had gotten her pregnant. Well, I was in the kitchen when she came to the party trying to talk to him about what they were going to do about it. She was hysterical and distraught because, you know, back then, it was a shame for a girl to get pregnant out of wedlock. You either got married, or you got sent away to the country. Anyway, he just told her to calm down, and he would talk to her later. He came in the kitchen acting like nothing happened. He wasn't even going to tell me about the girl, and I didn't say anything. Well, that night, he took me over to his house thinking he was going to get some, but when I wouldn't do it, he went to sleep. When he was sound asleep, I jumped on top of his stomach with a match in my hand. He felt the heat against his skin, and his eyes popped wide open. I told him I was going to drop it on him if he didn't tell me what was going on with Betty. He told me everything. I calmly explained to him that the next time he lied to Betty, or me for that matter, I was going to find him and put rat poison in his food." She laughed and then added, "It scared the shit out of him. He was so scared he married the girl two weeks later!"

"Did you ever tell Betty?" I asked.

"No. It wasn't her fault. She was my friend, and she was pregnant. I didn't want to hurt her any more than she already had been. I just decided to move on. I wasn't going to let Walter stop me, and a year later, I met your father and we were married."

"Mama, you never told me this. Why didn't you talk to us about stuff like this?"

Lisa, who was at our house more than she was at her own, added, "Yeah, Mrs. Davenport. We could have used this info to avoid some of the busters we've been dealing with throughout the years."

"See, that's the problem with you young women. You all spend too much time trying to figure men out. You can't figure men out anymore than they can figure us out. If you get hurt, you just have to keep trying until you find the person that's best for you. That's just part of life. The key is to keep trying. Don't get me wrong. All men are dogs. They're just different breeds. The key is selecting the right breed. You can pick a pit bull, a dog that could turn on you at any moment, or you could get yourself a German shepherd, one that will be loyal till the end. The choice is always yours.

"You're bound to meet bullshit ass niggas, but you have to deal with them in order to know what a real man is. And, when you meet a real brother, you'll know him. No mistake about it. You'll know him." With that, she was through with her portion of the conversation. My mother was like that. She talked when she had to, not because she could. She never said anything unless it needed to be said, and when she was through talking, there was no need in asking her anything else because in her mind the conversation was over. I appreciated that in her, especially now. I'd had my share of bullshit ass men, but now, it was time to move on.

Later on that night, I decided to figure out what it was that I was looking for that I wasn't getting out of men and my relationships. I devised a checklist of what I was looking for in a man. It went something like this:

_God-fearing ('nuff said).

_Strong (What is strong? Someone confident enough to be himself and humble enough to let me be myself).

_Honest (I'm sick of liars. Nathan was a liar. Please God, no more liars.)

_Ambitious (A man who has clear-cut goals and does what's necessary to accomplish them).

_Brave (Let's face it…no one wants a punk!)

_Sense of Humor (Please make me laugh. I've had enough pain in my life to last an eternity. I'm sick of crying. I want to laugh).

_Sensitive (He understands that sometimes I don't need to laugh. Sometimes I *need* to cry.)

_Faithful (If you say that I'm the only one for you then mean it! Don't cheat-period).

_Attractive (No one wants to wake up next to a booga wolf!).

_Intelligent (Make love to my mind, not just my body).

_Generous (Share–not just material things but your life, too. If you don't let me in, how can I know anything about you?).

_Financially Secure (Living paycheck to paycheck is *so* not cool. I need to know that you offer a place of security. I'm not looking for a sugar daddy, but I'm not trying to be a sugar mama, either!).

_Have an open mind (Can you try new things? Live life through new experiences–don't be stagnant).

_Supportive (Can you be my cheerleader and support my goals and ambitions?).

_Drug & Disease Free (Come on…Do I even have to explain this one?)

I knew I was asking for a lot, but this is what I needed *and* wanted from a man in order to be happy in a relationship. Yet, as I looked at the list, I started asking myself: *Do I possess the qualities that I'm looking for in someone else? How can I expect someone to provide these things for me when I can't reciprocate?* After Nathan, my faith was definitely shaken. In my current relationships, I wasn't letting anyone get close to me. I was too ambitious; I put my career before everything and everyone. I could definitely use help on being a better supporter. Nathan was proof of that. Although his busted ass did take advantage of me, what I thought was support was often nagging.

It was time for me to put the brakes on my love life in the serious sense. Lloyd, Kyle, Nathan, and Lorenzo and all the other brothers in between were not responsible for the woman I chose to be. Only I was responsible for that.

It was time I took time out and learned that, so that when a real brother came along I would be ready.

Chapter 16
The Bachelorette Party

Jaslyn, May 2003

"Hey, Jazz, Aunt Linda called last night. Girl, guess what? Tamika is getting married!" Melissa called one Saturday morning in May to tell me about our cousin's upcoming nuptials. Tamika Clemmons was my cousin on my daddy's side. When we were little, we used to play together and spend the night with each other all the time.

"Really? That's good news, but why didn't Aunt Linda just send an invitation?

"She called to invite us to the bridal shower and bachelorette party. The wedding is not for another month, so we should be getting the invite soon."

It had been a long time since I'd seen her, but I was really looking forward to seeing Tamika and her family. They were really crazy and liked to have a good time, so I was not going to miss out on any of the celebrations.

"When is the shower and bachelorette party?

"Tonight. Around seven."

"What! Why such a late notice?"

"Girl, you know how black people are…we ain't never on time. Anyway, are you going? You know you don't have nothing else to do," she said laughing.

"Don't start Melissa. Are you going?"

"Hell, yeah, I'm going!"

"What about Carol and Francine?"

"Carol can't find a babysitter this late, and Francine has to work the late shift. Are you going or not?"

"Yes, I'm going, Melissa, damn! Do you want to ride with me, or do you want to meet there?"

"We can meet up. I don't feel like listening to you bitch about me being late. They're having it downtown at the Worthington Hotel. It's in one of the suites, but she isn't sure what the room number is. Aunt Linda said to just ask for the Clemmons party."

"That's cool. I'll see you there, and you really need to work on being late…that shit ain't cute!"

"Bitch, bite me. You know…"

Click. I hung up on her. We could go on for days playing like that. I wasn't worried; I do it to her all the time. She normally just curses me out in person at a later time.

I had no problem dropping all of my plans to go to the party because I didn't have any plans. It had been two months since my birthday party, and my family's so-called relationship intervention. To a degree, what they did worked. I decided to take a sabbatical from men. I got rid of Vincent, and I refused to date anyone else. I hadn't had sex in two months and that included Spike. For me, that was a long time to go without sex. Vincent had been giving it to me on the regular for a about a year and half (how he explained his daily absence to his wife was unfathomable), and I was having serious dick withdrawals.

But I wanted clarity. I wanted to be free from all the baggage that was weighing me down and closing me off to positive relationships with men. I wanted to grow spiritually; all I did was meditate and exercise more. I had to exercise twice as hard to combat all the chocolate I was substituting for sex. I hadn't so much as gone to the club with my girls because I knew that would have been like taking a crack head to a cocaine factory–I *was* going to fall off the wagon.

My reprieve from men was the best decision I could have made because I was a much better person for it. I was beginning to understand that my issues with men were not the result of some inherent flaw in them, but it was part of a desire, some longing, I had to be complete. Being by myself made me realize that I didn't need a man to make me feel complete. I realized that what I was looking for was a complement, someone who complements my life, and I complement his. So when we're together, we're better people.

I was doing perfectly well for myself alone, and if fate decided that I was to spend my life that way, then I was satisfied. With understanding comes relief. You don't have the added pressure of trying to have someone to fulfill society's expectations of you even if that someone is not right for you.

I was comfortable with who I was now. I was ready to start having fun and going out again, and who better to do it with than my family.

I arrived at the suite at around 6:45pm, and to my surprise, everyone was present and accounted for, even Melissa. I heard Tamika before I saw her. Her booming voice and gregarious nature almost made you forget that she was only an inch over five feet tall. Always the center of attention, if she wasn't telling jokes, then Tamika was telling somebody's business. She was still the same. The only thing that had changed was the haircut, which framed her face in loose curls. Tamika's skin had a golden glow; she was beautiful. She had the unmistakable look of a woman in love. As I approached, I eyed her closely. Her head was thrown back in laughter. I knew for now that she was telling jokes, but it wouldn't be long before she was telling somebody's business. *What can you say? That's family.*

She spotted me and waved me over.

"Come on, Jazz! You made it just in time."

There were about twenty girls in attendance for Tamika's shower. We started the evening by having cocktails and eating hors d'oeuvres. After a series of icebreakers and games, the bride became the center of attention when she proceeded to open wedding gifts accompanied by complimentary oohs and aahs. She seemed to be elated with the blenders, towels, china, and lingerie she received from family and friends. Once the official shower ended and all the old people left, we headed to a local club that hosted male dancers on Saturday nights…we couldn't get freaky in front of old folks.

We were all having a good time stuffing dollars down the dancers' thongs and laughing at the bride's antics. She was so drunk that she tried to throw her own show with one of the strippers. Fortunately, her maid of honor escorted her from the stage before she revealed parts of her body that no one else wanted to see but her future husband.

The male revue ended around one in the morning but we all stayed at the club drinking and talking. Soon, the conversation turned to Tamika's wedding day and her fiancé. One of the bridesmaids asked, "So, Tamika, are you nervous?"

"No. It's about time Jawaan and I were married. I've been putting up with his bullshit for too long."

Everyone around the table gave their *Amen's* and *I-know-that's-right* speeches. Everyone, that is, except me. Melissa tried to stop me, but I had to ask. I assume she saw the expression on my face because she placed her hand on my arm and said, "Don't start, Jazz."

"What?" I asked as if I had no clue as to what she was talking about. But I knew exactly what she meant when she gave me that *You-know-what-I'm-talking-about* look. My family was good for giving facial expressions that let you know when it was time to shut up.

"Whatever, Melissa," I continued with my course of action anyway. "Tamika, if you know your man is full of shit, then why are you marrying him? Aren't you causing yourself drama for no reason? Forming a relationship that's destined to fail?" I looked at Melissa, and she shook her head knowing that from this point on there was no turning back from the can of worms that was about to be opened.

Tamika wasn't hearing it, "Oh, there you go with your intellectual ass! Always over-analyzing everything." She and Melissa and a couple of my other cousins gave each other high-fives and started laughing in unison. Tamika, however, was not finished with her answer to my question.

"Look, I know what I'm getting. With every man, there comes a certain amount of crap that a woman has to put up with. You just have to decide if that man is worth it and if you can put up with it. Jawaan's worth it, and I can put up with it. Pretty much, he just wants to hang with his stupid friends and not be nagged to death. I can deal with that. He has a great job, and he comes from a good family. Besides, we've been dating off and on now since the eighth grade."

"Wow! You've been together that long?"

"Yes, so I know exactly what I'm getting. In all relationships, you just have to know what you're dealing with.

But, since we're talking about marriage, when are you going to jump the broom?"

"That's not on my agenda at the moment."

"And why is that?"

"It's just not. If it happens, it happens. I'm not seeing anyone seriously right now, and I'm not going to worry myself about getting my hooks into some man. If it's meant to be, it's meant to be."

"So you're not seeing any one at all, right now?"

"No one."

"Not even that married man you were sleeping with?"

Where the fuck did that come from? I was taken aback. Not because she asked, because if anyone was going to ask a question that was none of his or her business, it was Tamika. I was startled because I had every reason to believe that my private affair with Vincent was just that–private. I had prided myself on how discreet I'd been in that particular relationship. *Nosy bitch.* "How do you know about that? And even if that alleged accusation is true, why are you telling my business in front of all these people? I don't know them."

"You know Fort Worth is small. We all know everybody's business, and we're all family here. No one has room to judge because we have all done our share of fucked up shit. Anyway, bitch, answer the damn question."

"Put the liquor down. You have definitely had too much to drink. To answer your question, no, I am no longer seeing him. I'm on a hiatus from men. I need to focus on me right now. Why?"

"Because Jawaan's best friend is single, and I think you might like him."

"Don't start trying to fix me up. I'm not looking for a relationship. My life is fine the way it is."

"That's exactly what he says to Jawaan when he tells him about you. You guys would be perfect for each other!"

"Girl, let's get you married before you start worrying about me. But, what's his name?"

"Sampson. Alicia you remember Sampson Tate, don't you?"

Alicia Matthews was one of Tamika's bridesmaids. We had just met that night, and the entire evening she remained aloof and cool. She was rubbing me the wrong way—something about her just wasn't right. Don't get me wrong she was gorgeous. I won't even try to take that away from her. She had it together. *Too* together. Her Prada dress, $400 shoes, and $200 hairstyle only added to the illusion of her perfection. Sometimes when the package is too flawless, it makes you wonder what there is to hide. She was pompous. The only reason we knew how much her hairstyle cost was because she kept telling us about her upscale salon and the stylist who only serviced local celebrities. I found myself wondering *Well, who is* **she** *and why is* **she** *here?* Throughout the evening, she kept looking at her watch as if she had somewhere else to be or something better to do. But who was I to judge.

"You mean the nerdy boy who used to like me? Girl, you don't want to talk to him. He's so corny," she offered as if doing me a favor.

"Thanks, but I don't want to date anyone right now. I'm happy being single."

Tamika would not be deterred. "Girl, Sampson and I don't get along, but he is *FINE!!* He owns an advertising firm; he has a condo, and he doesn't have any kids."

I was curious but I decided not to let on that I was interested. "No, thank you."

"Whatever. Don't slip up and miss out on a good thing. I don't care what Alicia says; she messed up when she let that go!"

Alicia continued the campaign against Sampson saying, "Shut up, Tamika. We were only in the eighth grade. You're the only heifer I know who hangs on to a man for twenty freakin' years. Girl, you don't want Sam. He's too sensitive and clingy. At least he was then. Maybe he's changed, but I doubt it."

I couldn't tell if she was trying to convince me or herself.

Part IV
Real Love

Chapter 17
The Wedding

The day of Jawaan's wedding we, did our usual thing. Played ball, got our haircuts, and hung out. We were pretty relaxed and well-rested. Jawaan refused to let us throw him a bachelor party. According to him, he had outgrown such shenanigans, but I believe that Malik's recent brush with the law had Jawaan scared. Knowing the party would involve strippers, I don't think he wanted to take any chances.

The wedding took place on a Saturday evening in June. In Texas, that meant that it was going to be a hot, clear day no matter what time the wedding started. Jawaan and Tamika were married at six in the evening at the Fort Worth Botanic Gardens. The location was the perfect setting for a summer wedding and reception. The ceremony was held in the Japanese Garden section. The wedding coordinator did an excellent job of arranging the chairs and decorations to blend with the natural setting. The aroma of the blooms was palatable, and the flowers provided a décor that could not be surpassed by the creations of man.

This day was important for Jawaan because it was the day that he stood before God and family, declaring his love for the woman of his dreams. On the contrary, I was happy being single. For the last few months, I was quite content with being alone, and I relished my freedom. While I was, ironically, reflecting on the joy I found in just being me, I also found the love of my life.

Jawaan had been trying to hook me up for a while with one of Tamika's cousins, but I wasn't having it. Tamika and I didn't get along because she had a *stank* attitude, and I was not about to put myself through that in a relationship with one of her cousins.

I don't know if it was the setting of the gardens or the romantic aura created from the nuptials, but when I met Jaslyn, I was completely overwhelmed. The wedding was over, and everyone was mixing and mingling at the reception in the pavilion of the Japanese Garden. I was talking to Jawaan who was getting ready to start the receiving line when she walked up. She wasn't very tall, but she had a confidence about her that made her seem gargantuan. She wore a beautiful halter-top dress. It was lilac with a bow that drew attention to her back and sexy shoulders. Her skin was mahogany, and she had deep brown eyes that bore through you and communicated her mischievous innocence. Her dark brown hair cascaded down to the nape of her neck, and her skin glistened in the evening sun.

I was looking good myself in my black, three-button tuxedo with a white silk shirt and tie. She was hot, and I was feeling her; I decided to show off. I loosened my tie and cleared my throat in anticipation that she was coming to talk to me, but she walked right passed me to shake Jawaan's hand and to hug Tamika, instead. *Can you say face crack?*

"Congratulations, girl! I'm really happy for you."

"Thanks. I can't wait for your day."

"Don't trip." They laughed together at their inside joke.

"Jawaan, this is my cousin, Jaslyn Davenport. Jaslyn, meet my husband, Jawaan Turner."

"Nice to meet you. Take care of my cousin, now. I know she can be a handful, but I don't want to call my peeps on you."

"Watch out, I got peeps, too!"

"I'm sure you do, but they're not as crazy as Tamika's family."

"You're right about that. I'll definitely keep that in mind." They all laughed, and I cleared my throat again trying to segue myself into the conversation.

"I plan on taking care of Tamika for the rest of her life. Don't worry, she's in good hands."

"Um–hum," I coughed a little louder trying to get my boy to get the hint. I'm sure he was prolonging the introduction on purpose–taking a secret pleasure in seeing me squirm.

"Excuse my rudeness," Jawaan said with a smirk. "Have you met my best man? This is Sampson, Sampson Tate."

She turned to me and extended her hand. "Pleased to meet you."

I took her right hand with mine, covered them both with my left, and shook it. Looking into her eyes, I replied, "The pleasure is all mine."

"Well, we'll see you guys later. We have to mingle with our other guests," Tamika announced just a little too loudly.

As they walked away, Jaslyn turned to me smiling.

"You know they've been trying to hook us up, don't you?"

"Jawaan did mention to me that Tamika had a cousin that he wanted me to meet, but he didn't tell me that you were so beautiful."

"Thank you. What a nice thing to say."

"It's the truth."

"I do apologize, but Tamika didn't provide too much information about you."

"That's a first. That girl is usually full of information, especially the wrong kind."

"I see you know my cousin quite well. It's true, though. All she said was that you owned an advertising firm and that you were fine."

"Now look who's saying nice things."

"It's the truth. I must admit that I should have had her introduce us sooner." This girl had me blushing.

"Let's find someplace to sit down and talk." Before we left, a waiter passed, and I grabbed two glasses of champagne for us. We walked out of the pavilion to the gazebo of the Rose Garden. Surrounded by shrub and tea roses and lily of the valley, the gazebo was the perfect place to talk without interruption. She sat on the ledge of the gazebo, and I positioned myself next to her. I thought it was the perfect setting we needed to get to know each other better.

"So, Jaslyn. What do you do for a living?"

"I'm a therapist at a women's shelter."

"Really, now. How interesting. What's that like?

"It's extremely rewarding. I work mostly with battered women, but occasionally, I conduct counseling sessions for the state with recovering addicts and ex-cons who are trying to re-integrate into society."

"I'm sure that's stressful!"

"It can be, especially if you develop a personal relationship with them; although professionally, that's frowned upon, but can be hard to avoid. Sometimes it's difficult to maintain your objectivity when these women so desperately want to be loved."

"Loved?"

"Yes. Many times, I find that the root of most abuse, self-inflicted or otherwise, stems from a desire to be loved by someone. Usually an absent parent but sometimes a parent that's present in the home but emotionally distant. Consequently, many of my clients lack self-love, so I try to teach them techniques and strategies to promote self-love and deal with their addictions."

"Does it work?"

"It all depends on the client and how accepting they are to change and growth." She paused to take a sip of champagne. "But, enough about me and my job, tell me something about you."

"What would you like to know?"

"Whatever it is that you want to share."

"Since we're talking about work, I'll start there. I started my company, Tate & Associates, three years ago. We started out with mostly smaller contracts, like the city's tourist bureau, non-profit organizations, grocery stores, and attorneys—things like that. I even did one of the Ernest McGhee commercials. You remember those?"

"You mean the guy who does promotions for local entertainers. Please, tell me it wasn't the one with Lil' Jimmy dancin' on the cardboard box? Oh my God, you must have been desperate!"

"Fortunately, we didn't produce that commercial, but yes, I was that desperate. His money was good, and honest, so I was taking it!" She shook her head in amusement.

"Within a year, we landed a contract with one of the city's leading producers of African-American hair care products, and things have been looking up ever since. Just recently, the firm negotiated a contract with a soft drink company, and we now have the exclusive advertising rights in this region."

"What exactly does that mean for your company?"

"How can I put this? Say one of my clients wants to do a commercial, maybe use an athlete or a celebrity of some type. Well, if that company wants to remain popular throughout the country, then it would be wise of them to market their products differently in different regions. Players popular down south are not necessarily popular up north and vice-versa. They would use a different player for the consumers in the north. It might even be music. We use a lot of Tejano music in Texas, but that might not work well in New York. So, my company's job is to create campaigns for the soft drink company that are geared specifically toward people in the southwest.

"It means lots of revenue for my company and lots of work for me, but I'm looking forward to it."

"How's it going?"

"Pretty good, actually. We just wrapped on a commercial and are about to run it by some focus groups in Texas, Oklahoma, and New Mexico."

"Congratulations on your success. I hope the commercial works out for you. So, are you seeing anyone?"

"Damn, you're direct! I like that."

"No sense in beating around the bush. I don't have time for that."

"Good. No, I'm not seeing anyone. What about you?"

Just as she was about to answer the question, Alicia Matthews walked up. She and Tamika had remained friends, and she was a member of the wedding party. How and why she found us outside, I don't know.

"Sam, aren't you going to dance with an old friend?"

I looked up at her in astonishment. I didn't have two words for this girl and here she was asking me to dance.

"I'm busy right now, Alicia"

"Oh, I'm sure she won't mind."

Now, here's what did it for me. Gracefully, Jaslyn conceded, "It's okay, Sampson. Go ahead. I've been monopolizing all your time, and I don't want to take you away from your friends. We'll talk later. I promise."

"At least walk back with us to the pavilion."

"No, that's okay. I'm enjoying the night air. You go ahead. I'll be going back to my family soon, anyway."

I danced with Alicia for two songs while she yammered on about Dunbar, and her accomplishments in college and society. When she started flirting and making references to us hooking up, I ended the dance by saying that I needed to go so I could give the toast for the groom. I headed back to the Rose Garden looking for Jaslyn, but she was already gone for the evening. I hadn't even gotten her phone number, and I didn't know much about her. That was okay. Tamika and Jawaan had hooked me up with a phone number before, and they would hook me up again. But this time, I wouldn't be a punk ass and have someone call for me. This girl had too much energy to leave it in the hands of someone else. I would call her personally and make sure she understood exactly where I was coming from.

Jawaan and Tamika were so busy I never got the chance to talk to them again. Before I knew it, they were in the limo headed to the airport to leave for their honeymoon.

Now, I would have to wait at least a week to get the information I needed. *Damn*, I thought. *I fucked up!*

Chapter 18
Renewed

Sampson, June 2003

Solomon was preaching his first sermon, and I was going to hear it. I was nervous. Not for Solomon. I knew he was meant to do this, and I was sure he would do an excellent job. I was nervous because I hadn't been to church in more than five years. It had been so long I was sure that Armageddon would begin as soon as I stepped across the threshold. I didn't even go on Christmas, Mother's Day, or Easter for fear that I would be labeled a hypocrite. Plus, it's always crowded on those Sundays, and I never felt the need to have people staring at me.

It had been a week since Jawaan's funeral. *Oh, I meant to say wedding.* I often called it his funeral because I was convinced Tamika would be the death of my best friend; although, I had given her a few more cool points since meeting her cousin. Jawaan hadn't called me yet, so I still didn't have Jaslyn's phone number. I told myself that if I hadn't heard from him by the end of the day, I would call him on Monday to get the info I needed.

Several weeks prior to meeting Jaslyn, I'd taken time off from women; therefore, I was being totally honest when I told her that I wasn't seeing anyone. To tell the truth, I really wasn't interested in dating anyone. I was enjoying my freedom, and I was getting in touch with Sam, a little self-induced therapy.

My therapy also included my spiritual growth. I was a stranger to the sanctuary, but I started praying again. I realized that I needed a one-on-one relationship with God. He was always talking to me, but I was never talking to Him. Through prayer and renewed faith, I eventually came to understand why I was longing to feel the love of a woman so badly. I would pray, then listen. My mother's image kept coming up.

The only memory I had of Sylvia Tate was on my fifth birthday. Aunt Tootie gave me a party at her house. My mother, Solomon, and I were living in the projects, and my aunt thought I would have a better party at her house. My mom went to the bathroom, and was gone for a while. Like any child who misses his mother, I went looking for her. When I opened the door to the bathroom she was sitting on the toilet with a needle in her arm. I saw enough dope addicts in the projects to know exactly what she was doing. Aunt Tootie was standing behind me. She walked by me and slapped my mother across the face. They argued, but eventually, my mother left and that was the last day I saw her. Sylvia Tate was the first woman to truly break my heart, and I craved that unconditional love that should have been given to me by her.

I realized it wasn't that she didn't love me. She just loved drugs more than she loved anything else—even her family. There wasn't any fault in me. The fault was in her. I hadn't seen my mother in over twenty years but I learned to forgive her. And, yes, to love her, for giving me life.

Now, I knew that I had that unconditional love from God, and I could stop looking for someone or something to fill that need. Sure, I curse. I still talk dirty, especially when I'm with my friends. I drink. I fornicate. I will probably have to always ask forgiveness for that particular sin. I don't think I'll ever be able to give that up…at least I'm honest about it, but I am a work in progress. As long as I kept striving to be a better person, it was okay to have imperfections.

This was the one thing that my brother kept telling me. When I started praying again, I started consulting him more, and he encouraged me everyday. We discussed the fact that I had not been to church in forever, and he didn't lie. He told me that I needed to go to at least fellowship with other believers. But, he also knew that it was important for me to return when my heart told me it was right and not because I felt pressured. We both agreed that his first sermon would be the perfect time for me to remind myself what the inside of a church looked like.

My conversations with God and my brother were providing me with a sense of clarity that I hadn't had in a long time. I was able to focus more and to understand my purpose better. I was also able to eliminate negative people from my life. Unfortunately, Malik wasn't one of them! He was my friend for a reason, and I was his. We argued all the time, but we were still able to be there for each other. I think that I was his conscience, and he was mine. So he was there to stay, and I was cool with that. There were women who continued to call me just for sex. I had not obliged; although, I was never able to completely sever those relationships. Through this renewal process, I made them see that I would no longer be, in the words of Eddie Griffin, their "man-whore." I also managed to fire a few employees who were not producing. As a black man, I always felt the need to help a brother or sister keep his or her job despite insurmountable evidence by these employees that proved they didn't want them. Most of my staff came in early, took working lunches, and stayed late to complete their assignments. Meanwhile, two particular employees were always late, took two-hour lunches, and still managed to leave early. I couldn't take it any longer. They had to go.

I felt a freedom that I hadn't felt in a long time, and that's what I was feeling the day I met Jaslyn. While talking to her, I didn't feel that my freedom was being encroached upon like I often did with some of the other women I had dated; consequently, I wanted to explore the connection that I felt with her. Screw Monday! I was gonna call Jawaan that night.

The day of the service, my entire family was there. Aunt Tootie managed to bring Uncle Junior. He stayed sober long enough to sit through the sermon; nevertheless, as soon as it was over, he headed for the liquor store. I wanted to leave almost as soon as I arrived. I was nervous, and one of the ushers only aggravated my anxiety when she held out her hand for me to place my gum in her pristinely white glove. I felt like a kid all over again.

Malik came with Womack and some of the other barbers to support my little brother's entrance into the world of evangelism. I must say that he was really good. He wasn't like these new-age preachers who gave what amounted to a motivational speech with very few references to the Bible. Solomon had that old-school gospel flair, but his message had numerous biblical references to give credence to the lesson. He had an uncanny ability to reach the most intellectual of parishioners as well as the common, hard-working church member who just wanted to hear the Word straight, no chaser. He broke it down in terms that everyone could understand, but it remained grounded in spirituality. My Aunt Tootie said that he brought the word to the world and not the world to the word. Meaning, he brought the message of God to change man and not the other way around.

It seemed to work, too. Despite the stifling heat, there were about twenty ceiling fans going, but it was still ten degrees hotter than hell in the building. I swear I saw Satan sitting on the steps of the pulpit. Solomon had the Amanda Street congregation on its feet shouting and stomping. The women started "catching the spirit" and passing out. I found myself thinking that they were really passing out from the heat, but I refocused on the sermon and tried to remain positive. I couldn't hear him for hearing "Yes, Lord," "Thank you, Lord," and "Preach, Brother" being repeated over and over, shouted, and screamed as if every word he uttered was the antidote to the misery of life, and the only way to get it was to yell for it. Malik and I, along with Chicago, approached the altar for prayer. His message had definitely worked on somebody's heart.

We left shortly before the service was over in an effort to avoid the third offering for the building fund. We all waited outside on the front steps of the church to talk to my brother. Malik and I were laughing at the usher who got "filled with the Holy Ghost" and started running up and down the aisles of the church. She made it to the front of the sanctuary and started hopping up and down, jerking back and forward with her arms stretched out wide. We thought a fight was going to break out when she hit another usher in the face as the woman was trying to fan her. Everyone knows in church when people "get happy," you leave them alone until they calm down enough for you to deal with them. Leave it to Malik to find the humor in a spiritual experience. I was still laughing when I felt a tap on my shoulder. I turned to find, to my chagrin, Brother Timms staring me in the face.

"Well, well, well, if it isn't Sampson Tate. I'm glad to see you made it to the service, today, son. It's been a long time." *Leave it to him to throw it up in my face.*

"Nice to see you, Brother Timms. How have you been?" I asked as I shook his hand with a smile that was as plastic as my uncle's leg.

"Just fine, son. I'll be doing even better if I can keep my young saints from back-sliding." He was still trying to front me out, and I still wanted to give his ass a beat down. Just when he was about to really make me feel guilty, I heard a soft voice behind me.

"Excuse me. Sampson Tate? Is that you?" I turned again, but this time instead of a bug-eyed face like Brother Timms, I saw the cherubic face of Jaslyn Davenport. *Damn, had I hit the jackpot or what?* Any woman that could save me from Brother Timms was definitely alright in my book.

"Excuse me, Brother Timms. It was nice seeing you again but I'll have to talk to you next week."

"So, you are coming back next week then?"

"Yes, sir. I'll be back next week." Damn, he still managed to get on my nerves, but I still had to respect him.

I turned back to Jaslyn and said, "Well, hello there, Angel. What are you doing here? Do you belong to this church?"

"My name's not Angel. It's Jaslyn."

"I know that, but you have be my guardian angel because you saved me from that demonic deacon!"

She laughed. "I'm sorry. I thought you forgot my name. And, no, I don't belong to this church. I went to school with the person who preached today."

"I'm surprised to see you. Actually, I'm rather happy about it. I thought I was going to have to arm-wrestle Tamika for your number since you left the reception so quickly. And you know I was not going to beat that girl in arm wrestling!"

"You are so silly."

"No, I'm not really. I'm just trying to impress you by making you laugh." She giggled again. I loved that she was willing to stroke my ego.

"So, you know Solomon?"

"Yes. We attended UTA together. How do you know him? Are you two related?"

"He's my brother."

"Small world! Your last names didn't even register."

"I'm about four years older than Solomon, and I went to UNT."

"He and I graduated the same year. We had a couple of classes together. I hadn't seen him in years. Then, I saw him last week at the wedding, and he invited me to the service, today. I'm glad he did. He was really good."

Just then Solomon walked up. "Jaslyn, I'm glad you could make it!" They embraced each other and let go.

"Thanks for inviting me. I really enjoyed the service."

"I see that you met my brother, Sampson. He's not harassing you, is he? You have to watch this one. He's not always for the right thing!" He joked, punching me in the shoulder.

"Not at all. We actually met last weekend at the wedding, and we were just reacquainting ourselves."

"Oh, really." Solomon got the hint and managed to find a way to leave us to ourselves. "Well, I see Brother Timms talking to Aunt Tootie. Let me go over and say hello before he has me flogged before the Deacon Board as an unfit preacher. I'll catch up to you later, Jaslyn. Sam, you still taking me out to eat?"

"I don't know. You eat too much."

"Whatever, man. I'll be with Aunt Tootie whenever you're ready." With that, he walked off.

"I guess I'll leave now so you can spend time with your family."

"Oh, no you don't! You're not getting away that easily. I let you use that excuse last week, and you got away from me. Not today, sister." In the bright Sunday sun, her dark skin shone like polished brass against her yellow dress. Her hair was pinned up, and it elongated her beautiful neck. Normally, I was not attracted to women like her, but she was confident, sophisticated yet down-to-earth, and intelligent. The fact that she was fine was an added bonus.

"You're funny."

"Look, girl, I like you, and I want to get to know you better. I would love to cook dinner for you this weekend. Would it be okay if I called you to set something up?

"That's fine. I don't know about coming to your house, though. You might be a serial killer." We both laughed.

"I am not a killer. Serial, or otherwise, however if you don't feel comfortable, that's fine. I'll call you tomorrow, and we can talk more about it. How's that?"

She opened her purse, pulled out her business card, and handed it to me. I'd have to tell Jawaan that my chicken-shit days were now officially over. I'd hooked this one up on my own.

As I watched her get in the car, I smiled, pleased with myself, but I also said a silent prayer: *Lord, please, don't let her be a manipulator or have STD's or have another man's baby or be crazy as hell. In Jesus' name I pray, Amen.*

Chapter 19
The Date

Jaslyn, June 2003

Sampson called on Monday, as promised, and we talked everyday that week. By the time Friday rolled around, I felt comfortable going to his place for dinner. Besides, I had given all his vital statistics to Lisa and Shelly just in case some shit went down.

I arrived at his condo at seven sharp. I hated to be late, anywhere, and I was not about to start with this date. I rang his doorbell, and within a matter of seconds, he opened the door. I was duly impressed. We decided to have a very casual date so that we could relax and get to know each other. Our first two encounters had been so formal that we wanted to just chill. The brother looked good in suits, but I must say that he could rock a pair of blue jeans like nobody's business. His jeans also gave me a good view of his butt. I'd always appreciated a nice set of buns, and Sampson did not disappoint me. Along with his dark-blue jeans, Sampson wore a short-sleeved, light blue V-neck sweater that accentuated his well-defined chest and biceps. A small portion of his chest hair peeked through the top of the sweater. It was jet black and curly just like his hair, and I wanted to run my fingers through it immediately. *Hello! Is your name Adonis?*

"Hello, please come in," He said. "You look great!"

"Thanks. So do you." I decided to wear a pair of sage green cargo pants that hung low on my hips with a yellow princess fit t-shirt that clung to my waist and played up my breasts. I was comfortable but sexy.

I stepped inside the door, instantly enjoying the cool breeze from his A/C instead of the heat from the sweltering Texas climate. I savored the reprieve from the heat. I glanced around to surmise the décor. His taste was contemporary and masculine, yet ironically inviting. The condo had an open floor plan so that the living room, dining area, and kitchen seemed to be one big room, but there was a bar that separated the kitchen from the dining area. He'd used deep earth tones to decorate each room with stainless steel appliances to accent the dominant pieces. The living room consisted of a leather couch in a deep walnut with two matching armchairs and a mahogany coffee table. It also contained a buffet style entertainment unit, which housed several books, small African artifacts, and various pieces of electronic equipment that were related to his flat screen television mounted above it. His dinette set was a long rectangular table in a warm brown finish. The side chairs continued the contemporary look with a diamond back design and deep cream seat cushions. The kitchen topped off the sleek, modern design with its glass front, cherry wood cabinets and granite counter tops. Sampson had a small collection of artwork throughout the apartment that provided a striking complement to his furniture.

"I'm glad that you made it okay. How was your day, Angel?"

"I was really busy, today, so I am definitely looking forward to dinner." I guess he'd already given me a pet name. I should have been uncomfortable with it; contrarily, I positively adored it.

"Good, because I threw down in the kitchen. You want something to drink until everything is ready?"

I laughed. "Thank you. Just some water for now."

"Girl, don't play. I didn't invite you over here so you could pretend like you don't have an appetite. I hate to hear women say 'I'm not hungry' or 'I don't eat that much'," he mimicked in a singsong voice imitating a high-pitched, coquettish woman. I couldn't help but laugh at his indignant discourse on the "prim and proper attitudes" of women. "Whatever you want, just ask."

"Whatever I want," I asked devilishly.

"Yes," he said walking toward the kitchen a few steps ahead of me.

"Anything?"

"Of course," he responded incredulously.

I lowered my voice to project a slight degree of sultriness.

"Are you sure about that?"

He stopped walking and turned to look at me.

"Oh, okay. So you wanna play. I'll say it again." He slowed down to enunciate his words. "Whatever…you want…I've got it…Just ask."

"I know exactly what I want," I said looking him directly in the eyes.

"And that is?"

"I want…" I walked closer to him stopping just inches from his lips. I drew in closer, our lips now millimeters apart. "Are you ready?"

"Yes," his voice was low and guttural. I was ready, and he was ready. It was time to stop playing. He closed his eyes.

"I want…," I said again, my voice barely above a whisper, "…a glass of water."

He opened his eyes, "What?" He looked at me as if he wasn't quite certain what he had heard.

"A glass of water. It's hot, boy! You said I could have whatever I wanted," I said innocently.

"You're crazy. You realize that, don't you? You are really crazy."

We both laughed and continued into the kitchen. He poured me a glass of water and continued preparing dinner. I stood at the island and watched him chop vegetables.

"How long before dinner will be ready? I'm starved."

"Thirty minutes. I'm glad to hear that you're hungry because for a minute there, I thought you were going to act all dainty and front like you don't eat."

"I'm not trying to front like that. I already told you that I was ready for dinner. What's on the menu?"

"Oven-fried catfish, grilled vegetables, rice pilaf, and for dessert, key lime pie."

"Sounds good."

"You can thank Patti LaBelle."

"I see you use her cookbook."

"Mmm–hmm, especially when I'm trying to impress people."

"You keep saying you're trying to impress me. Most men would never admit that."

"I'm not most men."

"Why?"

"Why am I not most men?" He talked as he chopped bell peppers, zucchini, and squash.

"No, silly. Why are you trying so hard to impress me?"

"I'm not trying hard, necessarily. I just want to make you feel special. I like you."

"Well in that case…I like you, too."

He stopped chopping to look at me. "We both like each other, so what are we going to do about it?"

"We," I paused, considering my words carefully, "…are going to take this slow. We're going to take the time we need to get to know each other and do this right, so that in the end, if all else fails, we can remain friends; hopefully, without all the drama that can ruin friendships and family relationships."

"True dat!"

"Since we are getting to know each other, though, let's play twenty questions. I'll ask you things women think about, and you can ask me things men think about?"

"Cool, fire away."

"I'm not talking about that superficial shit, either, like pet peeves, your hobbies, or your favorite color, or crap like that. Tamika gave me the low down on stuff like that when she got back this week."

He began sautéing the vegetables. I was glad because my stomach was starting to growl a little bit.

"You're spying on me."

"No. It's called research. Tell me she didn't tell you anything about me. I know she did because she talks too much."

"Well, actually she didn't"

"I'm shocked."

"Don't be. She told Jawaan, and he told me." We laughed. "How else would I know that you liked key lime pie?"

"I should have known. That girl can be so juvenile; it's ridiculous. Anyway, we'll ask questions that we really want to know the answers to. Can you handle that?"

"Sure, go right ahead."

"First question. Have you ever hit a woman?"

"No, but I sure as hell wanted to, though."

"Oh, Lord, Tamika has hooked me up with an abuser! Why would you want to hit a woman?"

"Because she hit me first. It was my ex-girlfriend. Don't get me wrong; I don't believe in putting my hands on a woman at all, but that girl pushed me to my limits. I broke up with her before I became a violent man. Just the thought of being with someone like that scares me."

"Why is that?"

"The thought of wanting to hurt someone you care about is frightening. I saw the way my uncle treated my aunt, and the effect it had on her was dismal. I used to wonder why she stayed. I hated him for the shit he did. It was like watching a wild animal attack its prey. Eventually, you have to kill that animal in order to control it. People only act like that because they feel trapped, when all they have to do is walk away. I never want to be like that."

We were both silent for a moment. I remembered the day I attacked Nathan. All of a sudden, I was ashamed of my pugilistic behavior, and I wished that I could rewrite history. I hoped he never found out that I could be that wild animal. Cornered and caged. I'm glad he didn't ask me the same question. I knew that I wouldn't be able to answer it truthfully.

"I hope I didn't overwhelm you."

"No, not at all. It's just a lot to think about, which is good. I'm extremely honored that you opened up to me.

"Okay, next question."

"Hold up. When do I get my turn?"

"You can go after I ask this question. How do you feel about children?"

"What heavy questions so early in our relationship!"

"Who says that we're in a relationship? We're just being prudent and cutting to the chase. You know, seeing where our heads are. That way, if we're not mentally on the same page, we won't waste each other's time."

"Kind of like getting rid of the middleman?"

"Exactly. Now, answer the question."

"I like kids. I know that I don't want any right now. As a matter of fact, I would be fine with not having any at all. But if I'm blessed with them, then hopefully, it will be with the woman I spend the rest of my life with. I grew up without either one of my parents. Although I turned out okay, I want to give my kids the opportunity to experience having a mother and a father. Kids have enough problems without adding single parenthood to the equation. Is that the right answer?"

"There is no right or wrong answer. I'm just trying to see if you feel the same way I do."

"Do I?"

"Possibly. Now, I want to know…"

He cut me off. "No, no, no. This is not the Spanish Inquisition. It's my turn now."

"Okay! Dang, you play hardball."

"And you know this! But back to the task at hand. Here's what men want to know."

"And that is?"

"How do you feel about giving head?"

"Daaammmnnn! Where did that come from?

"You said that I could ask questions that men wanted to know."

"But I meant important stuff…like family, friends, background…shit like that."

"In a man's world, gettin' head is very important. Stop stallin'. Answer the question."

"Your question isn't fair."

"Why not?"

"Because, if I say I'm down for it too fast, then I automatically get labeled as a hoe. You'll stay around long enough to get a blowjob and then go on about your business. If I say that I don't do it, then I get categorized as a prude, and there definitely won't be a relationship between us.

Hmmm…let me say this. With the right person and in the right time, anything is possible. How's that?"

"Now that was a good answer!"

I loved Sampson's sense of humor, and it was obvious that he was intelligent. We had a definite connection and were enjoying each other's company. We continued with dinner and asking our questions. He told me about Solomon, and his family, Jawaan, and Malik. I told him about my sisters, Shelly, and Lisa. We even went down the inevitable road of past relationships. I told him about Nathan, Kyle, and Lorenzo, careful not to mention my relationship with Vincent or my brush with the law while dating Nathan. He told me about Asia, Layla, and many of the women he had been dating over the years. He even told me about how he met Alicia and what happened the night of his eighth-grade prom. I laughed at the three-way phone call that Tamika and Jawaan set up for him and reaffirmed my dislike for the first girl to break his heart. We understood that we were in the same place, emotionally. Looking for love but trying to avoid being scorned. Before it got too heavy, we talked about our careers and family and it was good to know that those things were equally important to him as they were to me.

We talked about everything. Our love of music, books, and sports. I loved that one of his favorite songs was the Piña Colada song. You remember the song–*If you like Piña Colada and gettin' caught in the rain.* He sang it to me to prove that he knew all the words. He told me it was his aunt's favorite song. He used to hate it, but she used to sing it so much when he was a boy it eventually grew on him. I really laughed at that, and he laughed at me when he learned that my favorite movie was *CB4* and that I knew all the words to all the songs in the movie. He was speechless when I told him that I owned copies of the movie on VHS and DVD. I think I heard him mumble under his breath, "Unbelievable."

He was a great conversationalist and an excellent cook. The man had it going on in every sense of the word. He told me more about his business, and I expounded on the world of therapy and battered women. We even discussed religion, spirituality, and our decisions to cool our love lives until we were more centered and grounded. I was elated to see that we were on the same wavelength. Before the night was over, we agreed to get together in a couple of weeks to attend an outdoor jazz concert in Euless, a suburb just north of Fort Worth.

I decided to end the evening because Sampson's conversation was mentally stimulating, and I was extremely aroused. He was becoming unusually familiar to me in a short time period. I found myself inadvertently touching his hand or his arm. Or, he would allow his thigh to brush against mine as we sat on the couch. I'm not even going to go into clichés about electricity or any of that because I don't want to diminish its magnitude, yet the energy between us was definitely startling. Before I knew it, we were sitting snugly on the couch sipping wine, listening to the sultry sounds of Sade. His arm draped around me, he leaned over to kiss me. I returned the favor. It was a simple kiss. All lip and no tongue, but he was smooth enough to let it linger. Just enough to give me something to think about. And *think* I did. I thought about how nice it was. How good his lips felt and how sweet they tasted. I thought about how I hadn't felt a kiss like that in a long time. Not since Kyle. And that's when I knew it was time to leave. My body tightened, and Sampson felt the change in my attitude. He let me go to look at me.

"What's wrong?"

"Nothing. I just need to go home; that's all."

"It's late. You should stay here. It isn't safe for a woman to be on the streets this late." *The shit men will say to get some pussy,* I thought.

"It's only eleven. I'll be okay."

"It's closer to one."

"Oh, I didn't realize it was that late. I'll be fine. I know my way around. I have a conference to attend tomorrow, so I need to get home and get some rest. But, I have thoroughly enjoyed myself this evening. Thank you."

He walked me outside to my car.

"Thanks for the company, Jaslyn. I look forward to spending more time with you. Would it be okay if I call you this weekend?"

He was such a gentleman. Always asking would it be okay if he did this or would it be okay if he did that. I liked that shit! *Remember fellas, chivalry is a definite turn-on.*

"Of course. I look forward to it."

He pulled me to him and kissed me again. This time a little deeper and longer than the first. I found myself relaxing in his arms wanting more of his sweet, tender lips. So, I gave a little more to get a little more. Just as I was about to really enjoy myself, I panicked and my body stiffened. Again, he felt the change and released me. He kissed me on the top of my head, taking a few moments longer than was necessary in order to inhale the strawberry scent of my recently shampooed hair.

"Good night," he said. He opened the door for me to get in, and when I did, he closed it and stood there until I drove off.

On the ride home, I had time to reflect on what I was feeling. It wasn't just nervousness or fear. What I felt was quite physical. I felt my heart tighten in my chest, and my stomach became twisted in a knot. My lungs expanded, and my breathing became heavy and measured with anticipation. It was like having a panic attack. I knew what it was, though. It was the same feeling I had with Kyle and Nathan. It was the burgeoning feeling of love. I was falling for Sampson, and it scared the shit out of me. It was too soon for that. I hadn't felt that way about anybody in a long time, and every time I had, it was always followed by a disastrous consequence. I didn't want to feel that way ever again. I didn't want to relive that nervous, frightened feeling you get when you want someone, and you're hoping with all your heart that they want you, too. I had no desire to suffer through that horrible excitement you get when that special someone walks through the door, and you're glad to see him. You don't want him to know it, so you use that nervous, kinetic energy to pretend that you're busy.

I had it bad for Sampson; only this time would be different. This time I would follow my head and not my heart

and do the best that I could to prevent myself from getting my
feelings hurt.

Chapter 20
Love Calls

I knew Jaslyn was scared, so I held back on purpose. When I asked her what was wrong, I knew that she wasn't being completely honest. She may have had to work the next day, but that wasn't the reason she was ready to leave. She decided to leave because she was starting to feel something for me, and I was starting to feel things for her. Hell, that's the reason I kissed her. It felt natural. It was the most perfect and natural thing to do in that moment. We just had a vibe the entire night, so I went for it.

I knew what she was feeling the moment I looked at her face. It was the same look she gave me after I kissed her outside. That's why I didn't say anything. I didn't want to put her in a position to have to make up excuses or lie to me. Although we had shared many things that evening, I knew that she wasn't ready to open up to me on that level. Don't get me wrong. I wasn't disappointed by any means. I felt the date ended perfectly, and I admired her insight in monitoring her emotions. Most women would have been more than eager to tell me that they were in love or thought they were falling in love or cared for me or whatever was necessary to get close to me. Her hesitancy grounded my emotions, as well. It made me stop and reflect on what I was feeling, but at the same time, I was able to see that I needed to slow my roll. While I admired her perception, she still garnered major cool points for not taking advantage of a situation that could have easily been manipulated and for trying to mask her fear without appearing to be commitment-phobic.

We attended the outdoor jazz concert, which was cool, because it gave us an opportunity to have a picnic, with excellent background music, without it seeming pretentious. We continued to see each other and I never tried to take our physical contact beyond hugs and kisses. I wanted her–*badly*. She wanted me, too, but I would not increase the level of our intimacy until I knew that we were both emotionally ready to handle it.

Our dates were spontaneous and unusual. We did entertain with the obligatory dinner and a movie, but we often liked to be adventurous and try new things. She would take me to museums and to vineyards in Grapevine. I would take her rock climbing and fishing. She told me that she had never been fishing before and had always wanted to try it, so we started going out to Joe Pool Lake, periodically, to see what we could catch. One of our favorite things to do was to go to the library. She loved to read, and I did, too. We would discuss our selections and laugh at the bookworms who didn't have lives and were obviously there by force and not by choice. Sometimes, we would check out the erotic literature of D. H. Lawrence and read each other stories or marvel at the illustrations in the Kama Sutra. Because we were trying to hide our nervous anticipation about moving our relationship towards this area, we would treat the subject matter humorously by laughing like school kids until the librarian would threaten to kick us out for disturbing the patrons. But secretly…I was making mental notes of the positions I wanted to try with her later. All in all, taking it slow and getting to know each other was pretty cool. It was like Tantric sex…an extended orgasm!

About two months into the relationship, if that's what you want to call it because we had not given it a label yet, I met Malik for lunch. We had been hanging out together more often because Jawaan was still enjoying his newlywed status with Tamika and was not ready to leave the security of his home. We were cool with it. We understood his need to secure his nest, and we would be there for him when he returned. But, a by-product of his absenteeism was a stronger bond between us.

"Say, man, have you talked to Jawaan lately," he asked me as we ate lunch at Charleston's, a quaint little restaurant near Tanglewood.

"No, not in a while. Why, what's up?'

"He called me last night to tell me that he and Tamika are having a barbecue on Labor Day weekend. They want me to deejay."

"What?! I remember your bootleg deejaying days back when we used to go to house parties in Jawaan's Escort. How long has it been since you've done a party? Was it senior year? Can you still do it?"

"I'll never lose my skills. I told them I would do it. It's not like I have anything else to do."

"Maybe that could be a career option for you. Nothing small time. You could start a professional deejay service or something."

When Malik first lost his job, he was okay with it. He had a decent retirement plan and had invested his money well, so he wasn't hurting too bad for money. However, the emotional impact of being unemployed was beginning to take its toll. He was starting to get anxious about what the next phase of his career would be. Sometimes talking about it was a touchy subject, but today, he seemed to be ready to open up.

"Naw, man. I deejay for fun. That's not something I want to make a living from. You know with my situation and everything, I've been thinking about how much I love pussy. Sometimes I think I ought to be a pimp. Start my own escort service or something. The only thing that stops me is that I know I'll be using the services more than running the business."

"Are you out of your mind?!" I shook my head. Malik was unbelievable most of the time, but now, he was being downright ridiculous.

"I know. It seems strange for me to admit this, but I let pussy ruin my life. So, I started thinking that maybe I should take control. Make money off of trim instead it of making money off of me."

"Do you want to go back to jail? Man, you're just depressed."

"Boy, black people don't get depressed. We drink! And I've been doing it a lot, lately."

"Retard! Drinking is a sign of depression. Keep it up, and you'll end up like Uncle Junior."

"Oh, hell no! I just quit. Waiter, can I get a glass of water, please?"

"You're a sharp cat, Malik. Just get that dick of yours under control before you kill yourself behind it. Other than pimpin', have you given any thought to what your next move is going to be?"

"No, not yet. I really need to get on it, though. I'm doing okay, but my savings account is getting a little low. I'm about to start cashing in some stock, and I don't want to do that. What I really hate is not having anything to do. It gives me too much time to think about how I got in this shit."

"I can understand that, but don't let it get you down. You'll think of something. If you want, you know you can always come and work for me."

"Now, why would I want to do that? We argue enough as it is."

"True, but I just want you to know that I got your back. I can put up with your ignorant ass long enough for you to figure out what you want to do."

"Hell, no! I would never let you be my boss so you can order me around. Uh-uh!"

"Whatever, nigga! You know your broke ass need a damn job." After we stopped laughing, I added. "Besides, who says I have to be your boss. You could do some consulting for me. Corporate security. I need to a better security plan for my building, and I need advice on how best to secure confidential documents. You know, helping me secure my shit. You need to be your own boss, anyway. Who else is going to put up with your silly behind!"

"Now that's a thought. If I draw up a business plan, can you help me formulate a list of contacts?"

"No doubt."

"Cool, cool. I like that."

I was glad to see Malik's attitude take a turn toward the positive. He did some crazy things, but I still loved the brother. I felt bad seeing him down in the dumps. I decided not to talk too long about his career for fear that he would begin to slip back into his depression. I returned to discussing the barbeque.

"So, why is the dynamic duo having a barbecue?"

"I guess for the holiday. They need to do something since no one has seen them. They act like because they got married they can't leave each other for two seconds."

"Ain't that the truth! That brother is really whipped."

"No, you didn't. You really don't have room to talk."

"What are you talking about?"

"Man, you have no room to talk about somebody being whipped. Damn dog, all I hear you talk about is Jaslyn this and Jaslyn that. You can't shut up about the girl! I know we've been hanging out a lot lately, but you've canceled three times on me in the last couple of weeks. You startin' to act like a bitch. Her stuff must be the bomb!!"

I ran my hand across my face. I didn't know what to say. I took a drink of my beer and looked away from Malik while I gathered my thoughts.

"What, nigga! This broad has you speechless. Incredible!" He shook his head.

"I know, man. I know. I'm not whipped, though. Not that I want you all up in my business, but we haven't had sex, yet. To be honest, I like it that way. Don't get me wrong, I'm ready for it, but if she has me this caught up and we haven't even made love…damn. I just don't know."

"Sampson and Jaslyn sitting in a tree…," he sang like a kid in grade school. Before I knew it he was doubled over in laughter. "Whew! Sam is in love. What? Isn't this like the fourth or fifth time?"

"Your sarcasm is just not funny, alright. Don't hate on me because I've found someone, and you're sitting up licking your balls!"

"I don't need to lick my own balls. I got plenty hoes willin' to do it for me."

"That's what got your black ass fired in the first place. And for the record, I've only been in love one other time, and that was with Mrs. Mayfield. Alicia cheated on me before I got the chance to even fall in love with her. Asia did the same thing with horrible, horrible consequences," I said rubbing my groin. "And, Layla. That bitch was just plain off the wall!"

He shook his head at me. "You are *so* stupid! Mrs. Mayfield was fine, though. However, I noticed one thing."

"And that is?"

"You said, and I quote, 'I've only been in love one other time'. Does that mean you're in love with this girl."

"I'm starting to care very deeply for her, and I want to build a relationship with her."

"Does she know that?"

"I don't know, man. Look, she's not even my girlfriend. I don't know what to do."

"You know, Sam. All your life you've been a punk."

"What the hell?"

"You have. Must I remind you how you handled Alicia, Asia, and Layla? You never faced the truth about those women or dealt with them realistically. Be honest with this girl before you fuck this up, too."

"Is this the same Malik? Let's get the manager because I think they put something in your food. Could it be that you're ready to settle down in your old age?"

"Nigga, I'm nowhere close to being old. And, I will always be a playa. Always."

"I should have known that advice was too good to be true."

"No it wasn't. It's great advice...for you. Just let her know how you feel for once, instead of being a punk."

"That's the last time you gon' call me a punk."

"Punk!"

I kicked his leg underneath the table.

"Shit! That hurt!" He grabbed his leg, wincing in pain.

"I know it." I finished my beer and paid for lunch. " I don't know, man. I don't want to scare her off by coming on too strong, too fast. I want her to trust me."

"Then tell her that. Just be honest and build from there. The girl is diggin' you. I guarantee you that. But she's also the type of woman who doesn't give second chances."

For once, Malik and I seemed to be on the same page.

As Labor Day approached, I planned on addressing the status of our relationship with Jaslyn. Since my talk with Malik, I started building a plan of seduction. I recognized her anxiety in starting a new relationship, and I knew that all she needed was to be persuaded. That's all seduction is, right? The art of convincing someone to do what he or she didn't know they wanted to do. I flooded her office with flowers. I sent her e-mails and cards expressing my sentiments, but most importantly, I continued to open up to her. I let her in emotionally, which was really difficult for me; however, if I wanted her to trust me, I had to trust her first. We were seeing each other regularly, but we had yet to let our friends and family know that we were seriously dating. Malik knew because I was always with him. We wanted to keep what we had to ourselves until we were certain it was going somewhere. This way, if it didn't work out, our friends and family wouldn't be involved, and we all could part as friends. I was ready to change that, and I was hoping she was, too.

It was time to stop dodging the issue—it was time to intensify the relationship, and we both knew it. The weekend before Labor Day, I arranged for a limousine to pick her up when she got off work. He was instructed to take her to a local boutique where a personal shopper assisted her in picking an outfit for the evening. Once she finished shopping, I left a note with the driver explaining that she was to go immediately to a suite at an exclusive hotel where she was to prepare for the evening. After her bath, I had her hairdresser meet her in the room to style her hair. I wanted to be with Jaslyn, yet the ulterior motive was to try and relax her so she would have nothing on her mind. I didn't want any baggage from the day to hinder her willingness to give us a try.

While Jaslyn was in the bedroom getting her hair done, I had the hotel staff set up a candlelight dinner on the balcony. Her hairstylist was finished by eight o'clock, and when she stepped onto the balcony, I was standing there pouring her a glass of wine.

"You sure know how to make a girl feel special."

"It was nothing. Have a seat." I loved the way she dressed. She always chose outfits to flatter her figure. This evening she chose to wear a silk pantsuit in black with a sleeveless top and silver accessories.

"Damn, girl! You look good."

"Thanks to you.

"Take a seat and let me serve you." She did as she was told without protest. I prepared her meal and sat down across from her. The skyline and the light summer breeze was the perfect finish to a romantic ambiance. We finished our meal, and I was prepared to bring up the subject that prompted the dinner. However, she was one step ahead of me.

"What's all this about?"

"What do you mean?" I knew exactly what she was talking about, but I was attempting to circumvent the issue. I wanted to be the one to bring up the topic of our relationship. It was important that I remain in control of things so that I wouldn't back out of what I needed to do. Frankly, her brazen approach to the situation was a bit intimidating. Her attitude gave me a sense of déjà vu. Was she going to reject my advances the way I had done Catina? Karma can be a real bitch.

"Why all the fuss? The picnic. The cards. The flowers. The e-mails. The gifts. This dinner." She said waving her hand around the balcony to emphasize her point. "I am enjoying it, mind you, but where are you going with all of this?"

"I just wanted to have dinner with a friend. That's all."

"A friend, huh? Would you take Jawaan or Malik out for a dinner like this?"

"No…I wouldn't say that I would."

"So, this isn't just dinner with a friend, or they would be here and not me. Tell me, what is all of this supposed to mean? If it means anything. I know I'm taking a chance by telling you this, but I've been confused by this type of stuff before. And the truth of the matter is that I don't have time to be confused, anymore. People say actions speak louder than words. That isn't always true. I don't want to assume things that aren't there based on someone's actions. So, you need to tell me what this means that way we can both be clear about what's going on. If we're just friends, then that's cool. If you want to be more than friends, that's cool, too. I just don't want to get hurt because we weren't on the same page."

I sighed, carefully considering my words.

"You're putting yourself out there, and so am I. In a short time, we've become friends, and I look forward to being even better friends. But I want more than that. I'm starting to care about you, more than I care to admit. It's the truth. I know you've been hurt in the past. So have I. However, I'm willing to put my feelings on the line for a chance at happiness with you.

"Boyfriend. Girlfriend. You can call it whatever you want. Labels don't matter to me. Understand this. I want to be in a committed relationship. With you and no one else. You've opened up to me, and I've opened up to you. So, both of our feelings are in jeopardy. All I'm asking is that you give *us* a chance. Trust me." She looked into my eyes as if she were searching for signs of genuineness and sincerity. The verdict was still out. I waited. Breathing hard and apprehensive on the inside but maintaining my cool on the outside. We sat silently for a few moments. Finally, she took my hands in both of hers and kissed them.

I said, "Now. Are we on the same page?"

"Definitely."

"Then, I say we celebrate the inauguration of our relationship by attending Jawaan's Labor Day barbecue, together."

"I was already going."

"But, you weren't going as my date. I don't want to keep our relationship a secret any longer. Now you'll be going as my woman."

"Woman, huh? I feel the shackles clamping down on me already."

"Yes, woman. You know that's what you need. Someone to handle you with a firm hand," I teased.

"Uh–oh! I might need to change my mind about this commitment thing. You're already changing."

I stood up, walked around the table, and pulled her in my arms.

I whispered in her ear, "You don't want to do that now, do you?"

"No." She looked me in eyes and then she kissed me. I walked her to the bedroom. I removed her clothes and turned down the bed. She was kissing me and caressing me. I took her hands and placed them at her side. I kissed her again.

"Get in," I commanded. She climbed under the covers and reached up to kiss me again. I placed my hand on her shoulders and gently forced her against the pillows. I took the sheets and placed them under her arms.

"What are you doing?"

"I'm tucking you in."

"I'm a grown woman. I don't need to be tucked in. Aren't you staying? "

Her aggravation was funny, but I answered her calmly. "No."

"Why, not?" She was breathless with passion, and it was hard for me to resist her, but I had to.

"This night is for you. We have plenty of time to make love. But, tonight, I just want you to relax."

"I can relax any time. I want to…"

"Shhh. Get some rest."

I wanted to get in that bed and do things to her body that were unimaginable, but tonight wasn't about getting in her panties. It was about building trust. I needed her to know that what we said, what we agreed to, was real and not some underhanded attempt to sleep with her. I needed her to understand that I planned on being in her life for a while, and the best way to do that was to exercise some self-restraint. *Lord, please let me be the man You would have me to be and not the man I want to be. Amen.*

I gently kissed her goodbye and then reached for the lamp to turn out the light.

.

Chapter 21
House Party

We arrived at the party around three. The day was bright and sunny. Tamika and Jawaan were barbecuing to celebrate their nuptials and to thank family and friends who supported them during their engagement.

When we pulled up in Sampson's truck, he circled around to open the door. I took the opportunity to check out his physique and wardrobe. The boy was looking good in his faded jeans and dark-blue cotton shirt. I loved looking at his body. He wasn't slender, and he wasn't really buffed up, either. His body was well maintained on his 200 lb. frame. Always the gentleman, Sampson followed closely behind, but his real motivation was to check me out, too. I wasn't mad. I knew I was looking good in my khaki capri pants and red tunic. I added an extra swish when I walked. I was trying to make him regret leaving me hanging in that hotel room.

The party was in full swing when we arrived. Jawaan and his father had ribs, chicken, and links on the grill. Tamika and the women were in the kitchen with the women tending to the potato salad and baked beans. The house and backyard were filled with a mixture of Jawaan and Tamika's family and friends, fellowshipping and enjoying a well-deserved break from work. The celebration would not have been the same if Tamika's grandparents weren't sitting under the shade in lawn chairs eating watermelon and screaming at kids running through the backyard. The atmosphere was friendly and relaxed, an excellent combination for a blossoming romance.

When Sampson and I walked in, the shock was clearly registered on Tamika and Jawaan's faces. Although they knew we were interested in each other, they had no idea that our relationship had become serious.

"What's up, playboy? Where you been?" I overheard Jawaan ask Sam while I was in the kitchen with Tamika.

"My playboy days are over, J."

"Yeah? You kickin' it with Mika's cousin?"

"Yeah, man."

"That's good. She's fine as hell! I'm happy for ya, man."

I shook my head with laughter as Sam replied, "Thanks."

Just as Jawaan finished, everyone left the kitchen and headed for the backyard except for Tamika who turned around and let me have it.

"You heifer! I see you saw something in Sam after all. We've been home for two months; why didn't y'all tell us?"

"Because you talk too much, and we didn't want everyone all up in our business!"

"Bitch, whatever. So, how long have you two been seeing each other? Do you like him? Have you done the nasty? Fill me in, girl. You owe me something since I hooked y'all up!"

"You didn't hook us up. We hooked ourselves up. And I told you, I'm not telling your ass anything. You have a mouth like an old refrigerator; you can't keep nothin'!"

"You're right, girl. If you tell me, I'm gonna tell somebody," she said as we laughed.

I looked outside and saw Sampson waving at me to come outside. I walked out to him, and we made the rounds, socializing with family and friends. He introduced me to his Aunt Tootie and Uncle Junior. I was a little nervous because I knew how much she meant to him, and I wanted her to like me.

"So, Miss Jaslyn, tell me how you met my Sammy," she inquired with an air of haughtiness. Something was wrong; I knew I was in trouble. Sampson tried to deflect the ensuing conflict.

"Forgive her, Jazz. She can become extremely protective when it comes to her nephews.

"Aunt Tootie, please don't call me that. I'm a grown man. You make me sound like I'm two years old instead of thirty-two. And this is Jaslyn's first time meeting you. Leave her alone. You don't need to know all that."

"Boy, you are never too grown for me to take you over my knee. I'll call you whatever I *want*, and I'll ask her anything I *want* to make sure she's the kind of woman who's good enough for my nephew." She rolled her eyes and looked at me directly.

I knew the program, but my mother taught me better than to get an attitude or be disrespectful to my elders. I remembered a piece of advice she once gave me. Whenever I told her that I had a conflict at school, she always told me to kill them with kindness. So, I turned on the charm for Aunt Tootie. I smiled at her sweetly, then said, "It's okay, Sam. She loves you and is just looking out for you. I understand completely.

"Miss Camille," I added addressing her the way young ladies in the south were taught to speak when wanting to show respect to older women, "I met Sampson at Jawaan's wedding and Tamika is my cousin. Although we haven't been dating that long, let me assure you that I care about your nephew deeply, and I have the best intentions, which I hope he has towards me. If you're worried about the type of person I am, I can only demonstrate in time what type of character I'm made of. But if this helps, I'm thirty years old. I have a master's degree in Social Work. I'm a therapist for a women's shelter, and one day I want to start my own group home for abused women. I own a home in Arlington, and I just paid off my Volkswagen, which allows me to place a considerable sum in my savings account every month. So, I hope you see that I am not looking to get anything out of Sampson as some women might. I enjoy his company, and I hope that will leave room for you and I to get to know each other as well."

When I was finished, Uncle Junior replied loudly, "Ooh, I like her, Sam! Where did you find her?" This only seemed to enrage Aunt Tootie more, but she didn't say anything. Sam pulled me close and kissed me on the cheek.

Despite the heated exchange, I was having a wonderful time, and I felt comfortable being with Sampson and his friends. He walked over to the DJ booth to talk to Malik while I continued to talk with Aunt Tootie and Uncle Junior at the patio table. She attempted to be cordial to me, but I still felt a bit of the disapproval from before. Uncle Junior, however, was the exact opposite. He talked to me continuously, telling me jokes and embarrassing stories about Sam as a kid. He wasn't at all the way Sam described him, but then again, he was sober, which makes a big difference.

As we talked, I hummed on along to the music that Malik was playing. He served up a continuous play of old school cuts with an interesting blend of hip-hop and R&B, which made the evening so much easier. No one wants to be at a party with horrible music. Everyone was dancing and talking, but I was hesitant. Sam's rejection of me that night at the hotel had me guessing, and I was still trying to figure him out.

Malik played Erykah Badu's "Back in the Day," and it just suited the evening. Before I knew it, I started bobbing my head and singing along. When I looked up, Sam was standing in front of me with his hand out. I placed my hand in his, and he led me to the center of the patio; we started grooving together. At first, we were just doing our own thing, but pretty soon, we developed a rhythm together. Before I knew it, he grabbed my hand and began leading me in what my mother used to call the "swing out." Some people call it swing dancing but she used to say, "White folks swing dance. We swing out. There is a difference." And there was. This dance was not just about moving to music or leading and following. With the right person, this dance was about sensuality and seduction. It was communication. He drew me in and then pushed me back. He pulled me back in and then pushed me back to swing me around. His moves were saying, "I want you. Do you want me too?" When I relaxed my body and allowed myself to follow his lead my reply was, "Yes, I want you, too."

I used to hate this dance because I hated to follow. I always wanted to lead, and it would throw the rhythm off with my partner. However, Sam was totally in control. I liked that. He had the ability to lead me without me knowing I was being lead or that I needed to be lead. *Had it been that I had been following the wrong partners?*

Pretty soon, everyone stepped aside to watch us do our thing. When the song ended, everyone clapped and yelled,

"Encore, encore," like they were at some sort of play. Malik's crazy behind gets on the mike and says, "Go 'head wit yo' bad asses! I think I'll play that again." And he did, so we danced again. This time, everyone joined in. Sampson pulled me close, and we just stayed that way, dancing close and enjoying the nearness of each other as the music faded into Marvin Gaye's "After the Dance." The lyrics wafted through the evening air. We danced, hips swaying from side to side. He kissed me. We had been doing a lot of that, lately. I was ready for more. I couldn't take it anymore. Our thighs touched, I began to feel his manhood grow, and my body began to throb. "Let's go," I moaned. We left the party without saying good-bye and headed for my house.

Chapter 21
After the Dance

Damn, I thought we'd never leave! I couldn't contain myself. If I'd had my way, we didn't need to leave the party at all. The bathroom or a hall closet would have been perfectly fine for what we needed. But Jaslyn was calling the shots. Jawaan lived in Mansfield, which wasn't that far from her home in Arlington. We made it to her house in fifteen minutes, but it seemed to take forever.

When we arrived at her house she, quickly unlocked the door, and we rushed in. She locked it back, and we converged on each other in a heated embrace; our bodies intertwined in steamy kisses. Her lips entreated mine to engulf them over and over. Before I knew it, we had found our way to her bedroom completely naked, insatiably partaking of each other. We stopped for a brief moment for her to put on an Isley Brothers CD.

In an instant, she began to dominate me and take control. She straddled me against the mattress asserting control over her dominion, and I willingly acquiesced.

As we lay down on the bed, she kissed my lips. Light, soft, quick kisses. Then she kissed my cheeks. Then my neck. And then, just lightly on my collarbone. Then my chest. She kissed my mouth, again, but this kiss was deeper and more urgent. She started to break away, but I wouldn't let her go. I wanted to taste more of her, so I continued to kiss her. For a few moments, we just kissed and enjoyed the taste of each other. But soon, she gently broke away from me to explore more of my body. Her hands gently kneaded my chest and shoulders. She pulled me up to her, and her hands reached around me to caress my back, as she did, she nibbled gently on my earlobe. Her tongue started to dance in and out of my eardrum, and I was intoxicated. I couldn't think straight. I tried to call her name, "Jas…" but she stopped me. "Shhh…," she said to squelch my protest.

Jaslyn's hands urged my body back against the bed, and she began kissing me, again. Then, she formed a trail of light, feathery kisses along the rest of my body. First, on my chest, then my stomach, lower and lower until she found what she was looking for. She tasted me and liked it because she went for more. Her tongue flicked lightly against my flesh until she placed my penis in her mouth. Up and down, she moved. Slowly and methodically until I felt a deep, low groan escape my chest. I was ready to explode, and Jaslyn sensed it. She stopped just in time. She returned to my chest to kiss me again and stopped. Jaslyn was about to lower her self on top of me, but I was through playing games with her. Jaslyn had been in control, and she had shown me ecstasy. Now, it was my turn to play.

I pulled myself up on top of her. Now, she was under me, and I could see her body in its entirety. Her voluptuous curves were soft and inviting, but I was not quite ready to enter her. I wanted to touch her mahogany skin, so I did. I massaged her nipples, and then I took one in my mouth. As my tongue flicked back and forth across her nipple, Jaslyn began to purr. One by one, I allowed my tongue to feast on her breasts until I was satisfied, and she was trembling with pleasure. Her nipples were not enough for me. I wanted to experience all of her, so I tasted her the way she tasted me.

I licked her navel and every inch of her stomach. I got up on my knees and lifted her right leg to me. I kissed each toe, then her knees, and when I was done, I massaged her calf and kissed it as I moved toward her inner thigh. I spent several moments kissing her thighs, teasing her as I came close to her womanhood but refusing to close the deal. This was heavenly torture for both of us, and I was not ready for it to end. Soon, I lowered her right leg, lifted the left leg and performed the same routine in reverse. Light, feathery kisses on her thighs, calf, knees, and then each toe. Jaslyn was squirming, and deep, low groans were escaping her lips. She arched her back, and I knew she was ready. I was prepared to consume my meal. I lowered myself for the entrée. I placed my face in between her legs. My tongue darted in and out of her body. I found her clitoris and massaged it until she moaned in pleasure. She started squirming, arched her back again, and her thighs tightened around my neck and shoulders. She started to cum on my face, and I licked it up until every drop was gone.

I sat up and placed Jaslyn on my lap. I wanted to see her face. I wanted to know what she looked like when she came. "Get the condom out of my jeans." She complied, unwrapped it, and slid it over my dick without further instruction. We moved to the edge of the bed, and I entered her. I started moving slowly, in and out of her. My hands were on her hips as I moved back and forward and guided her to move with me. We moved deeply, passionately, until our breathing increased with our lovemaking. Back and forth. Back and forth, I moved. My body ached, and I was in pain. My pace quickened. We moved and moved, and moved. I felt her squeeze her thighs, and her pelvic walls constricted around my penis. I wanted to scream.

Her pussy was tight and warm; I didn't want to ever leave it. I moaned with pleasure. I saw her contorted face, and she chanted over and over, "Oh God! Oh God! Oh God! ...Please don't stop!" And I didn't. Then suddenly, I felt her body tremble. I increased my pace to match hers until I came so hard that I felt the vessels in my brain tighten and dilate like I was about to have an aneurysm.

We fell into each other, breathing heavily with exhaustion. We could have stayed there forever, like that. But finally, I kissed her and brushed her hair back. As we lay down together, I felt my heart beating in my chest. My eardrums were popping from the release of pressure. My post-coital skin felt icy-hot from the sweat that covered my body and the blood that pulsed beneath the surface. Finally, my heartbeat returned to its normal pace and my penis shrank to its original size. It was in that moment, I knew she was the one.

Chapter 22
After the Morning After

Jaslyn, The Next Morning

Finally. Finally, I've found the guy! Yes, **the** *guy. The man Lloyd told me about so many years ago when I was seven. My mother was wrong. All men are not dogs because clearly I have found one that is in a word—perfect. Yes, he has flaws, but he's the perfect person for me. We blend together so well. He's what I've been looking for—my complement. Finally, I can let all those guards down that I've built up over the years. I can relax. I'm in love, and I couldn't be more elated. Now, I know what Terry was talking about when she said to exhale. I'm relieved. What's a girl to do with all this happiness? I don't know if I can handle it.*

Those were the thoughts that ran through my mind the morning after Sampson and I first made love. I wouldn't tell him about my feelings, though. It was too early for those types of endearments, but I knew it. I knew I could open myself up to this man. He had it all. He was educated, financially secure, caring, sensitive, and spiritual. And the sex. The sex was all that! What more could a girl ask for?

The first thing I wanted to do was call my sister, Carol. My sounding board. I needed her to tell me that I wasn't losing my mind. That I wasn't crazy for falling for a man that I had only been seeing for a few months. True to my old pattern, I started second guessing myself. *Was it the sex? Was it so good that it had me thinking I was in love?* I was hoping that it wasn't. *Was it because I went on a hiatus from men? Had I spent so much time away from men that the first guy I encountered afterward would seem like he had it all even though he didn't?* I was hoping that wasn't true, either. I really liked this man, and I wanted what I felt to be real. I needed my sister to help me provide some clarity so that I didn't romanticize something that felt so extraordinary but was so, so ordinary.

When I got home that morning, I gave Carol a call on her cell phone. When she answered the phone, I opened up with my usual salutation. "Hey, girl. What's going on?"

"Nothing, much. I'm just dropping the kids off at school. Why? What's up?"

"Nothing. Can't I just call to chit chat?"

"You can, but you don't. I rarely hear from you unless it's in the middle of the week or there's something wrong. So, what's the problem?"

"It is Tuesday, so, maybe nothing's wrong."

"But it's seven in the morning, a time when you are usually dead to the world since you don't have to be at work until ten. I don't know why you're beating around the bush. Just tell me what's the matter."

"I don't even know where to begin." I was stalling because I didn't want to sound like a pure idiot. *What was wrong with me? Why did this man have me so discombobulated?*

When my pause lasted a moment too long Carol interjected. "You must have met somebody."

"How did you know?"

"The subject of men is the only area that gets you this confused."

"Who says I'm confused?"

"Girl, get a grip! This is Carol. You don't have to front with me. It's too early in the morning, and I don't have time. I have to drop my kids off at school. Why don't you just tell me what's wrong? You obviously know I won't judge you, or you wouldn't have called me."

"Okay, you're right. His name is Sampson."

"His name sounds familiar."

"He was in Tamika's wedding, and we've been seeing each other for several months."

"And?"

"I'm falling in love with him."

"Why do you say that?"

I filled Carol in on all the details of our relationship, thus far. Then I asked her, "Am I crazy? Isn't this too fast to be talking about love?"

"I wish I had a definite answer for you but I don't. There's no such thing as a timetable when it comes to your heart. Love is crazy. It's a crazy, crazy game we all play. We have to play. It's the essence of who we are as human beings. All you can do is give it your best shot, and if it doesn't work out, then start over."

"Well, that's the problem."

"What?"

"Starting over. I can't do it any more. My heart can't take it. I'm just not that type of person. I've been hurt too many times in the past. Relationships you don't even know about. If this doesn't work out…I just can't take the chance of it not working out. I just can't take it anymore."

"Do you want it to work out?"

"Yes."

"Then you make it work. Love is not easy. It's extremely hard. It requires an enormous amount of trust, determination, and work. You have to be determined to make the best of it, if you are both willing and able. Just give him a chance. You know you want to. And, be honest about your feelings with yourself and him. If he doesn't reciprocate, then move around."

My phone clicked.

"Hold on, Carol," I said and answered the other line.

"Hey, girl! Where you been?" It was Lisa.

"What are you talking about?"

"We called you last night, and you didn't answer your phone."

"Shellie? I know you two didn't call me to try to charge me up?!"

"It's not a charge. Just an inquiry."

"But Shell, you notice how she didn't answer the question."

"That's because she was out last night skanking it up!"

They both burst out laughing.

"Y'all hold on." I clicked over. "Carol, I'll call you later. This is going to take a while. And thanks for the advice"

"No problem, girl. Call me anytime."

When I clicked back over, Lisa and Shellie were launching a full-scale inquiry on my whereabouts from the previous night. Shellie was really letting me have it.

"You know she was with some man because she didn't answer her phone at home or her cell phone."

"She had to really be getting her groove on because she didn't even check her messages. I left her a message at home and two messages on her cell phone, and the skank still didn't call me back. I could have been dead." They were so involved in the conversation they hadn't noticed my return.

"Now, why must I be a skank, Lisa? And what was so important that you had to leave me all those messages?"

"Oh, shit. Girl, I was just playing."

"Whatever. You just got busted. It's too early in the morning to be messing around. What you heifers want?"

"Speaking of early. Where have you been all night?"

"None of your business, Shellie. Why are you so nosey?"

"I'm not nosey. Just concerned. No one knew where you were last night, not even your mother, and that's not like you."

"You called my mother! I cannot believe you. You know how she is. She thinks because I live alone I can't function. She probably called all of my sisters and started asking them, 'Is Jaslyn over there?' Shit, I am grown. Can't a girl get some without her family and friends throwing a search party?"

Lisa had finally stopped laughing and was re-engaged in the conversation. "You need to stop tripping. You know the routine. If we haven't heard from your ass in two days, and we haven't, then we come lookin'. That includes calling your mother. Bitch, don't play."

"Yeah, Jazz. Don't be so testy. I'm just glad you got some ass. After kicking Vincent's behind to the curb, your attitude was getting pretty hard to deal with. So tell us about it girl. Was it good? Who was it with?"

"You two are just regular comedians, huh?"

"Mmm-hmm. Abbott and Costello. Now, spill the beans," Lisa urged.

"Shoot, there's just no getting around you guys. Look, one of my cousins fixed me up with her husband's friend. "

"What's his name, and where is he from?"

Again, I retraced the steps of my relationship with Sam for Shellie and Lisa, as I had done with Carol. They were astounded that I had kept my relationship with him such a secret.

"Why didn't you say anything?"

"Lisa…I don't know. I just wanted to make sure that this was real, you know. I get excited about these relationships, and then they blow up in my face."

"So you guys are serious?"

"Yes. I really like him. If things keep going the way they have been, we may have quite a future ahead of us."

"Well, good. You deserve it."

"Okay, he's a good guy. Blah, blah, blah! You guys are so serious; let's talk about what's really important," Shellie rambled on. Then she asked, "What's he like in bed?"

"Mind ya business, tramp!"

"That bad, huh?"

"To tell you the truth, the shit was so good I forgot my name."

"For real?"

"Girl, I woke up this morning and thought my name was Jane. Or was it Joan? See, I still can't remember. I had to look at my driver's license. Mmph."

"Damn! For a minute there, I thought he was going to be as bad as the last guy I slept with."

Lisa and I both asked, "And who is that?"

"Girl, it was so bad I don't even want to tell you his name. Let's just call him 'Asthma'."

I knew better than to entertain Shellie when she was on a roll; it could only get worse, but I had to ask.

"Why Asthma?"

"First of all, when I met the dude, all he did was talk shit about what he was going to do to me in bed and how I was gonna be climbing the walls and shit. Y'all know I don't back down from a challenge, so I was like, 'Okay, we can do this.' Girl, before he could even get it in good, he was moaning and shit, talking about, 'Ooh girl, you sure do have some good pussy!' While I'm laying there thinking, 'I haven't even done anything, yet,' he comes."

I hollered, "Stop lying!"

"Girl, yes. And that's not the kicker. I started thinking, 'Okay, the brother is nervous,' so I gave him another chance. He did the same thing, girl. I was too through. Again, I got these questions going through my mind. I'm like, 'Did I miss something or is this shit I over?'

"Before I knew it, the brother was wheezing and grabbing at his throat. I'm like, 'What's wrong?' And he says, 'I have asthma.' Talking about 'I can't breath…I need air.' The stupid ass forgot to bring his inhaler, so I had to put him in the bathroom, turn on the shower, and let him inhale the steam. I just kept praying 'Lord, please let this fool live long enough for me to get him out of my apartment'. Can you believe that shit?"

After Lisa and I stopped laughing, I said, "Girl, you are so damn silly!"

"Whatever. I knew my shit was good, but I didn't know it was that good!"

December 2003

"My cousin is coming over to spend the weekend with me. I was wondering if you would come over this weekend and help me keep her company?" Sam called me at home. We had been talking for about twenty minutes when he put in his request. It seemed that he wasn't sure if I would come. "She's in college, and her mother thought I would be able to give her some encouragement while she was on break. I figured it would be better if she also had a female opinion. What do you say?"

"Sure, no problem." He seemed hesitant about asking me, so I added, "You sound as if you didn't think I would come."

"I wasn't sure, really."

"Why?"

"I don't know. We've been dating for a couple of months, but this whole relationship thing is still new. I don't want to ask too much of you."

"Spending time with you and your family is not asking too much, and it's not like you asked me at the last minute. I've got the whole week to prepare, and I don't have anything else to do this weekend. What time should I be over?"

"She gets in around five in the evening. How about seven or eight? That'll give us about an hour or two to catch up before you get here."

"That's fine. I'll be there at eight."

"Thanks, Jazz. I really appreciate this."

"Boy, shut up. We've been going out for months, now. Why wouldn't I help you? You are so crazy." I was playing hard, but I was smiling on the inside.

"I just want you to know how grateful I am. I don't want to take for granted that you would automatically help me because I know you don't have to."

"I want to help you, Sampson."

"I know. So, thank you."

"You are very welcomed."

"Sssooo, what are you doing right now?"

"Right now? Right now, I am getting ready for work tomorrow and running my bath water."

"Do you want me to come over and scrub your back?" I finally picked up on the lascivious tone in his voice.

"Mmmm. That would be nice…but only if you can stay. I'd hate to rush you."

"Believe me, angel, I won't rush. I always, always take my time."

"That sounds promising. Let me think about it."

"Think, hell! I'll be over in twenty minutes."

I chuckled. "Give me an hour. I need to straighten up."

"I could really care less about what state your place is in. I'm coming over there to handle my business."

"Oh, believe me, we are definitely going to handle it! But, every time you're here, you never really see anything because we head straight to my room. It's still early in the evening, and I would really like to give you a tour this time. You said this relationship wasn't going to be just about sex, so prove it. "

"I always want to spend time at your place, but I thought you just preferred coming to mine. You're the one that always acts as if have something to hide. I want the tour; I just don't know if I can wait that long."

"Anticipation is a natural aphrodisiac. Plus, I have to make sure I have the whip cream and chocolate syrup."

"Girl, you a freak!"

"I will neither confirm nor deny that accusation, "I deadpanned.

"And, you're demented too! I'll be there in an hour."

I put the phone on the receiver and went into a panicked frenzy trying to get the place in order. I had my nephews and niece over the day before, and the place was still a mess. It was like a bad episode of Benny Hill. Books were everywhere. I put them on the shelves next to the fireplace. When I ran out of room, I put them in the hall closet. I scurried from the living room to the hallway to my bedroom picking up clothes and placing them in the hamper. I took ten minutes to vacuum and dust. Then I lit scented candles throughout the house and put Eric Benét into the CD changer. I jumped in the shower and gave myself a quick shave. I scrambled out of the shower, dried off, and oiled my body until it was moist. Finally, I slipped on my lingerie and robe. Just as I finished, Sam was ringing my doorbell. Before I answered, I double-checked myself in the mirror. I sprayed on a bit of perfume and put on some lip-gloss. Everything checked out, so I went to answer the door. He was standing at the door in a pair of black Nike sweats and a white t-shirt. *Damn this man gets finer every time I see him!* I felt the throbbing begin in between my legs, and my mind raced—*Ooh shit! Just the sight of him makes me horny. Okay, girl, control yourself. Play it cool, play it cool.*

"One hour on the dot. Did I ever tell you that I like your punctuality?"

"No, but people are always on time when they are going someplace they want to be. Aren't you going to let me in?"

"Sure. I'd like to officially welcome you to my humble abode."

Sam stepped off the porch, walked though the door, and looked around. He gazed over my sage green overstuffed sofa and love seat with the matching throw pillows. He walked over to the fireplace and inspected the photographs on the mantle.

"This you?"

"Yes. I was in the third grade."

"Nice ponytails. You were cute."

"You say that like I'm not cute, anymore." I teased. I tried to ease the tension by being flippant and sarcastic.

"You're not. Now, you are beautiful." He looked at me, and I glanced away nervously. I felt like a schoolgirl.

He walked into my dining room and looked at my oak table and china cabinet. Next, he entered the kitchen, glanced around, and walked back out.

"Nice crib."

"Thanks."

"So, are you going to show me your bedroom?" He was blunt, and I was glad because I was sick of that fake-ass tour.

"I thought you'd never ask."

I led him to my bedroom with the expectation that this time would be better than the rest. I wasn't disappointed.

Tara, Sampson's cousin, was an exceptionally bright young lady who'd earned an academic scholarship to the University of Arkansas at Pine Bluff. This was her first time away from home, and she was having a difficult time adjusting. Her family lived in Dallas, and Pine Bluff was a relatively small city compared to a huge metropolis like Dallas. Her grades were good, but her mother was afraid because Tara was extremely homesick and constantly talked about leaving school to come back home. Sampson's sole purpose in allowing her to visit was to convince her to stay in school, and I was his accomplice.

While Sampson prepared dinner, I sat down with Tara to talk with her, privately, about the situation.

"So how is UAPB?"

"School is fine, but I am ready to come home."

"Why?"

"There's nothing to do in Pine Bluff."

"Didn't you get a full scholarship?"

"Yes, ma'am."

"Please, don't call me ma'am. It's perfectly fine if you call me Jaslyn."

"Okay."

"What I was trying to point out is that you went down there to get an education. A free one at that. Most people don't get that type of opportunity, so take advantage. Let me guess. You haven't made any friends, have you?"

"No, not really."

"Girl, make friends! Choose them wisely, mind you, but friendships are the best part of college life. Before you know it, you'll be less homesick. Sometimes, you won't even want to come home."

I proceeded to tell her about my friendships with Lisa and Shellie. How we studied together, partied together, starved together, and cried together. How they helped me through problems and situations that I couldn't share with my family. I told Tara about the road trips we made to step shows in Austin with no money and no clue as to how we were going to get in. How Shellie often flirted with someone at the door to get us in for free. Without telling her all the details, I couldn't help but share with her how they helped me to get over Nathan's infidelity.

"I could not have made it through college without them, and we are still friends to this day. They're still my girls and I love them as much as I love my own sisters. Give it a chance. Don't give up. Remember, Dallas will always be here when you finish school."

"Thanks for the encouragement, Jaslyn. It really helped. If you don't mind, I'm gonna call my mama and tell her that I am going back next semester."

Tara went to the back to use the phone, so I went into the kitchen with Sam. I walked up behind him and grabbed him around the waist. I stood on my toes to blow in his ear.

"I see you're thinking the same thing I'm thinking but hold off. I can't walk in front of my little cousin with a hard-on."

Before I could respond, the phone began to ring.

"Don't answer the phone. It's probably for Tara. Her friends from Dallas have been calling since she got here."

"I thought she was on the phone with her mother."

"She's probably using her cell. Just let the answering machine get it."

I began nibbling on Sampson's ear, again, laughing at how ticklish he was when the machine picked up.

"Hello, Sam. This is Alicia. I was just thinking about you. Give me a call so we can hook up."

I abruptly stopped nibbling on his ear and immediately dropped my arms from around his waist. He turned toward me and searched my face. I tried hard to conceal my thoughts. I knew I wasn't succeeding, so I started to walk out of the kitchen.

"Jaslyn, wait." He grabbed my arm gently before I could walk away. "It's not what you think. I haven't heard from that girl since the wedding. Before that, it had been years. I don't even know how she got my number."

"It's cool. You don't have to explain."

"Yes, I do."

"Why do you think you need to explain?"

"Because I know what you're thinking."

"What am I thinking?"

"That I'm lying."

"Now why would you say that?"

"Because it's written all over your face. Believe me, it's nothing."

"Okay, it's nothing. I believe you."

"You do."

"Yes." We both knew that *I* was lying. I just wasn't sure if he was or not.

We finished the weekend without further incident, but the seeds of doubt had already been planted in my mind. The following Wednesday, Sampson came by my house to watch a football game and have dinner. We were sitting in the living room in front of the television snuggling on the couch.

During a commercial break, Sampson turned me toward him.

"I need you to listen to me, Angel."

"What is it?"

"I know how Alicia got my phone number."

Instantly, my shoulders tensed up, and I dropped my eyes, not willing to show him the doubt that dwelled there.

"I told you that you didn't have to explain. I believe you."

I tried to get up from the couch, but he pulled me closer to him and whispered, "I know I don't have to explain, but I should. You said you let it go, but that doesn't mean you really let it go."

"Okay, then, how did she get your number?"

"My Aunt Tootie gave it to her. She saw us dancing at the wedding, and when the girl called her house, she thought that it would be okay."

Okay, that was believable. I knew his aunt didn't like me from the barbecue, so she was probably more than happy to pass his number along to some other woman. But, I thought back to the night of the bachelorette party and the evening of the wedding. I thought of the interest I saw in her eyes.

I asked, "So why is this girl coming around all of a sudden?"

"I don't know. She's silly. I guess she wants to be friends again, but I don't care. I don't want anything to do with her. She even stopped over to my house yesterday. She said she was in the neighborhood. Aunt Tootie gave the damn girl all my info."

"What happened?" The game was back on, but we continued to talk.

"Nothing. After I told her I was busy, she asked me if she could use the bathroom. I let her go and then she left."

I mulled it over and finally declared, "Well, you didn't have to explain, but I'm glad you did."

"I'm not crazy. I knew what was going through that suspicious little brain of yours." He had no clue as to how suspicious I had become. I tried to trust him, but the doubts were growing bigger and bigger.

He kissed me on the top of my head. He knew I loved it when he kissed me in my hair. He said, "Are you coming over this weekend?"

"I'll be over Saturday. Lisa and I are taking Shellie to Louisiana for her birthday. She wants to gamble to celebrate, so we're driving to Shreveport on Friday."

"The infamous Lisa and Shellie. When do I get to meet them?"

"You know I've been hiding you from them. They're crazy. I have to really like you first before I let you around them. They'll try to rake you over the coals, that's after you pass the background check!"

He laughed, and I finally said, "I'll have them drop me off at your house Saturday night and you can meet them then. Do you mind taking me home on Sunday?"

"Of course not. What time will you guys be back?"

"After seven."

"I'll be there."

While we were spending more and more time together, our relationship was still fresh, especially the committed part. It seemed as though the minute we promised to be faithful to each other, our trust, at least mine, was promptly tested.

The next day, Sampson and I had our first argument.

It started when I was in his bedroom looking for a t-shirt to put on. I opened the top drawer of his dresser and froze.

I called out to him. "Sam! Can you come here for a minute?"

He walked into the room.

"What's up?"

"I'm going to ask you a question. I promise I will not get upset. Just answer the question, please."

"Okay, Angel. What is it?" He looked confused probably because we had just finished making love, and he couldn't quite figure out why I had such an attitude.

"Whose underwear is this?" I held up a pair of black thongs.

"They're yours."

"If they were mine, would I be asking you who they belong to? Good answer but try again."

"They've got to be yours because they sure in the hell ain't mine!" He actually sounded believable.

"YOU KNOW THESE AIN'T MY FUCKIN' PANTIES!!"

"Okay, first calm down. I'm not just gon' let you scream at me like that. And stop crying."

It was too late. The tears were coming down before I knew it. I couldn't stop. I couldn't believe that he was already cheating on me.

He pulled me in his arms and began gently stroking my hair. "Calm down, Jazz. If they're not yours, they have to be Tara's. You know she was just here. They must have gotten mixed up in the laundry. Calm down, baby. Please calm down."

Sampson did his best to appease me, and I eventually regained my composure. He had a rational explanation, so I believed him. I wanted to believe him. I needed to believe him. I fell asleep that night in his arms hoping that these growing suspicions were truly unwarranted.

But, the fat lady sang on our relationship the day I came back from Shreveport. I called Sam to let him know that I was on my way back and was headed toward his place. I was looking forward to seeing him. I had spent the weekend listening to the continuous bells of the slot machines, fending off old men trying to fondle me, and listening to the cackling banter of friends in a shared hotel room. My head was pounding, and I couldn't wait to lie next to Sam and let him massage my shoulders, back, and feet.

I called his home and cell phones. When he didn't answer, I left messages. Despite our exclusivity, I still wanted to respect his space. He didn't call me back. Since we had discussed me coming over, I didn't think it would be a problem. When I pulled up to his condo, I realized that he probably would have wanted me to wait until he called back.

On a cold December evening, Sampson was standing on the steps with some girl draped all over him. Locked in what was clearly a lover's embrace, her arms were clasped around his neck, and he was holding her firmly around the waist.

Lisa asked, "Where is Sampson's condo?"

"You're right in front of it."

My friends gasped.

In a split second, I had to decide what to do. Do I get out and confront the situation head on? Do I get out and pull a ghetto girl move, curse his ass out, and slap the shit out of him? Been there, done that. I wasn't trying to go back to jail. This time, I would have to call my family to get me out because Shellie and Lisa would surely be going to jail with me. There wasn't a doubt in my mind that they would back me up.

While I was deciding my course of action, Sampson was finally able to pull his eyes away from her face long enough to notice that I had pulled up. When he saw me, he dropped his head and muttered, "Shit." I wasn't the only person whose thoughts could be read by the expressions on their face. He had shock and disappointment written all over him. He was shocked to see me and disappointed that he was busted.

Everything was happening in slow motion. Things that were happening in split seconds seemed to drag on forever. The young lady turned to see what had taken Sam's attention away from her, and at the same time Shellie was asking, "What you wanna do, Jazz?"

I recognized Alicia the moment she looked at me, and all my suspicions were confirmed. I refused to embarrass myself in front of a man who so clearly wanted to be with someone else. My answer was clear. I looked at Shellie and Lisa and quietly announced, "Go home."

202

Chapter 23
What's Really Going On?

"Man, whose panties are they?"

"I have no idea."

It was Sunday morning, and I felt sick to my stomach. *How in the hell did I get myself in such a mess?* I tried to reach Jaslyn last night after she left, but she wouldn't return my calls. I had no idea what to do. Out of sheer desperation, I phoned Malik to help me figure out what was going on. I couldn't talk to Jawaan because I wasn't sure if he would tell Tamika and I wasn't willing to ask him to keep secrets like that from his wife. I brought Malik up to speed on all the details. Of course, he focused in on the panties.

"You didn't tell Jaslyn that you didn't know who they belonged to did you?"

"No. I really thought they belonged to her, but when she said they weren't, I lied. I told her they were Tara's."

"Good."

"I know. I just wish it were the truth."

"Huh?"

"I called Tara, and she said they didn't belong to her, either."

"What? I thought you were falling in love with this girl. You steppin' out on her, already?"

"Naw, man. That's just it. I haven't done anything. I really don't know who the panties belong to."

"Finish the story. Maybe we can figure something out."

I recounted Alicia's unexpected visit, which I didn't mention earlier because he stopped me when I got to the hidden underwear, and Jaslyn's reaction when she pulled up.

"She was throwing herself at me, man. Trying to kiss all on me. I'm not feelin' her like that. I tried to explain to her that we knew each other as kids and that we were totally different people now.

"When Jazz pulled up, I was trying to push her off of me."

"Don't lie, Sam."

"Now why would I lie to you? I know it sounds unbelievable. I'm sure Jazz is thinking the same thing you are. I saw it in her eyes. I didn't know what to do or say because I knew she wouldn't believe me."

"Once a trick, always a trick. Why did you let Alicia come over to your house? She did you dirty once. Why on earth are you letting this girl come back around?"

"I'm not letting her come around. She just keeps popping up on her own. She's been calling me at home and at work. The first time she came over, she just showed up on my doorstep with the excuse that she just happened to be in the neighborhood. I didn't believe her. I wish to God that Aunt Tootie had never given her my numbers and address."

"Did you let her in your house?"

"Yes. She had to use the bathroom?"

"You idiot! Those are her panties."

"I never slept with that girl! How could her underwear wind up in my house?"

"She planted 'em."

"Nooo. Why would she do that?

"Boy, I swear sometimes you're stuck on stupid. She's getting rid of the competition. It's obvious she wants you, and Aunt Tootie, or Tamika, has probably been blabbing to the girl about your relationship with Jaslyn. You know that girl and her family have always been uppity. She probably found out about your business and money, and now, she wants to get with you. If she's trying to get you back, then she's just doing what she has to do."

"Fuck that trifling bitch! I hate the day I ever saw her ass."

"Don't be mad now, nigga. That shit won't help. I told you before that Jaslyn is not the type of girl to give second chances. You need to try to fix this before she writes you off completely…if she hasn't done so already."

"You're right."

"You said she drove off without saying anything. She just drove off?"

"Yes. Not one word."

"That's bad. Real bad. Now you don't know what she's thinking. If she had gotten out of the car you could have explained the situation to her."

"No, shit. Tell me something I don't know."

"Get slapped, alright? You called me, remember?" He paused trying to think of a solution. "There still might be a chance. Call her. If she doesn't talk to you, or she doesn't call you back that means she's still pissed. If that's the case, give her a few days to calm down and then go talk to her. Women can easily ignore you if they don't have to look at you. But seeing you in person is another story. This'll give her time to cool off, too. If you go over there now, she'll probably kick your ass. Besides, this way you let her know that you didn't just leave the situation alone, but you are giving her some space. Trust me. I know what I'm taking about. As many women as I've fooled with, I've had plenty of practice.

"Before you do that, though, you need to talk to Aunt Tootie and tell her to stop giving that girl all your personal information without your permission. I know she means well, but that shit ain't cool, man."

Malik was right. So, we finished our conversation and I headed to Stop Six. My Aunt Tootie wasn't home, but I decided to wait on her. Uncle Junior was there, and for a change, he was sober. I guess he had a lot on his mind or felt the need to talk because he usually leaves when I show up. Today, he stayed and actually inquired about my life.

He was sitting on the sofa in front of the television watching re-runs of *Sanford & Son*. I sat down in the recliner across from him. I didn't want to sit right next to him because he was still in his undershirt and boxers, and his prosthetic leg was leaning against the armrest of the couch. I know it's wrong, but that plastic leg always made me feel weird.

He looked at me smiling. "How's it going, Sam?"

"Fine, how are you?"

"Can't complain. What's bothering you?"

"Why do you think that something is bothering me?'

"Because you are actually talking to me and not dismissing me like you usually do."

"Frankly, Uncle Junior, you're normally drunk, so I never have too much to say to you. But if you must know, I need to speak with Aunt Tootie about someone."

"It's that girl, ain't it?"

"What girl?"

"The girl from the wedding. The one who stood you up at your middle school prom."

"Yeah, how did you know?"

"She's been callin' here everyday milkin' Camille for information about you. I told her she don't need to be tellin' your business like that."

"She didn't listen to you?"

"Hell, naw! Camille don't listen to me. Never has. That's why I drink so damn much. It's hard for a man to pay rent and feel disrespected in his own home."

"Look, this ain't true confessions time. Don't try to blame your alcoholism on my auntie. More than likely, you were drinking before you met her."

"You right. But it got worse after we were married."

"So are the cheating, abuse, and illegitimate children her fault, too?"

"No. I don't blame Camille for anything. The drinking, the cheating, the kids, and the abuse. They're all my fault. Your auntie was a strong-willed woman, and I didn't know how to talk to her or treat her. In my eyes, she challenged my manhood. I was old-fashioned, and when I felt like she wouldn't submit to my will, I tried to get her to obey me the best way I could. So, I would drink to build myself up to face her. You know there's nothing like that liquid courage to make a man feel like he owns the world. Alcohol gave me the power to say the things I needed to say and do the things I wanted to do. But when it got in my system, my judgment wasn't the same. Whatever I said was cruel and mean no matter what it was. It helped me sleep with people I had no business sleeping with and treat Camille in a way that no one should be treated."

"I wonder…what brought on this sudden epiphany? Why are you telling me all of this now?"

"You asked for one. Solomon for another. Talking to him has made me aware that I've been wrong for a long time, and it was time for a change. In a man's old age, he wants to be respected. You boys never respected me. Hell, my own children don't even know me. Praying with Solomon helped me see that I needed your respect and that it wasn't too late to get it.

"I could tell from the barbecue that Jaslyn is a good woman. Strong-willed, smart, and beautiful. Just like Camille used to be. That's why Camille don't like her. Jaslyn reminds her too much of the past. I don't know what you did to mess up but do whatever you can to fix it. She's too good of a woman to lose. Women like that don't come around often. So, don't mess up like I did with Camille.

"I don't know what you did to mess up, but when you go back to try and fix it, just remember that women are looking for adoration. They want someone who adores them. Every woman wants it, no matter what they say. Even the most scandalous of women will get dressed up in a skin-tight dress and strut at the club just to see a man's eyes linger over her body and hear him say 'Damn she looks good'," he said chuckling.

"So have you stopped drinking?"

"Huh! Son, Rome wasn't built in a day, as they say. Let's take one thing at a time." I shook my head as he laughed and said, "I'm tryin', though. I'm tryin'."

"Thanks, Uncle Junior." I felt bad, so I added, "Look, man, I love you. I just…"

"You don't have to lie, Sam. I know how you feel and I'm not angry about it. The way you feel about me is all my fault. What matters now is that we have something to build on for the future. Don't worry about me. And don't worry about Camille. I'll tell her to back off and this time she's going to listen. You just take your ass out of here and fix the shit you done got yo'self in!"

What the hell? Thank God for miracles. My world was turning upside down. The best relationship I had ever been in was about to end before it even started; my aunt whom I adored, was doing her best to destroy my happiness, and my Uncle Junior, whom I detested, was doing his best to keep it in tact. My mind was a smoky haze. After talking to Junior, I wanted to head straight to Jaslyn's house, explain everything, and declare my love. Yet, I knew her. I knew that she wouldn't believe me. In her eyes, I was a criminal in the court of love, and the circumstantial evidence was stacked against me. What was I supposed to do? I had to gather my defense. The first step, the plea. I called her. I dialed her number from my mobile but as Malik predicted, she didn't answer the phone.

"Jaslyn, if you are listening to this I hope you will hear me out. I don't want to talk about this over the phone. I want to explain everything in person. It's not what you think. I would never do anything to hurt you, but you have to give me a chance to explain. Right now, I need you to trust me. Do you realize that we have spent our entire lives not knowing how to trust anyone? It's time we learned how to trust someone. Why not each other? I love you, Jaslyn. Just call me."

I'd done it. I entered my plea, gave my opening statement, and closing arguments all in one message. I prayed. *Uncle Junior, I hope it works.*

Chapter 24
Cleaning House

I got Sampson's message, and as you probably guessed, I didn't return the phone call. He had called every day, but I refused to talk to him. My answering machine was inundated with his messages, but there was really nothing for me to say. Nothing for us to talk about. What could he say to explain that he was found in the arms of another woman? His first love for that matter. Just as easily as I had entered his life, I was leaving it. I spent the week grieving for the end of our relationship. You know the usual pity party. For several days, I called in sick to work, I stayed in bed, sobbed over the obligatory pint of Blue Bell, unloaded all of my emotional bullshit on my girls. By the following Saturday, I was sick of myself, and I was ready to move on.

That morning, I got up, threw on some sweats, a sweater, and a jacket. I had decided to go for a ride. Despite the overcast sky and icy temperature, I managed to get in my full three miles before the rain started to pound steadily on the pavement. This would have been another perfect day to be depressed and lick my wounds; nevertheless, I refused to be sad any longer. Upon my return, I showered, washed my hair, and slipped into a pair of blue jeans and a white t-shirt. I had the heat turned on while I was gone so the house was comfortably warm. I pulled my hair back into a ponytail in order for it to dry naturally without getting all puffy and frizzy.

The pigsty I called home was no longer tolerable. It was time to clean house. I went to the kitchen and grabbed my cleaning caddy and then grabbed the vacuum out of the hall closet. No Saturday morning cleaning session could begin without the perfect music to motivate you. I loaded the stereo with my favorite CDs: Jill Scott, Angie Stone, and Anthony Hamilton. I pushed random play on the CD player and let the music begin. Before I knew it, I was dusting, polishing, and wiping. I swept the floors and then vacuumed. The place needed a thorough cleaning. While vacuuming, I saw a stain that I wanted to remove on the living room floor. I had a bad habit of spilling soda or juice, so I was an expert at removing carpet stains. Somehow, I had missed this one.

I grabbed the Windex and a scrub brush. I sprayed the stain with the glass cleaner until it was soaked and began scrubbing. When I was little, my mother used to wake us up on Saturday mornings to the sounds of Earth, Wind, & Fire or Natalie Cole. My sisters and I didn't even have to ask questions. We knew what time it was. It was time to clean up. She must have known the therapeutic qualities that cleaning up while listening to good music on a Saturday morning had for you.

When I started cleaning, I didn't want to think about anything. I didn't want to think about the fact that I had missed a week of work. I didn't want to think about the length of my "to do" list when I returned. And, I didn't want to think about the cause of that list. Sam. I was sick of thinking about him. All I wanted to do was clean. I began scrubbing, but the more I scrubbed, the more I thought about Sam and all the relationships that led me to this point. Jill's voice rang through my head as her CD shifted into rotation. Something about her voice pushed me to scrub harder and harder as I thought about all the pain many of the men had caused me and the pain I had issued in return. I kept thinking *Why, Why, Why?* And my answer was continuously *Me, Me, and Me.* I deserved more than this. I was forever selling myself short. My relationships were bad because of me. I was always trusting too much or I was always trusting too little. *Something was wrong with me.* This relationship was supposed to work. It hadn't because I trusted him too much. I didn't want to give Sam the opportunity to hurt me again. I was getting angrier and angrier, so I scrubbed harder and harder until the stain was lighter than the carpet. Before I realized what I was doing, I heard his voice over my shoulder.

"I think the stain is gone."

"How did you get in here?" I wasn't frightened. I didn't even turn around to face him. In the back of my mind, I must have expected him to be there.

"I knocked, but I guess you couldn't hear because of the music. I tried the door, and it was open. So, I came in."

I still refused to face him. "Didn't Aunt Tootie teach you not to come into someone's home without permission? It's called breaking and entering."

We were both unusually calm.

"She did. Breaking and entering is a small price to pay compared to the crime I'm really being accused of. And, didn't your mother teach you not to have your ass all in the air with the door unlocked? If I weren't the man I am, I could have run in here and had my way with you. Don't be so careless."

"How thoughtful," I said, my voice reeking with sarcasm as I stood up and turned to face him. Sarcasm was my only weapon. I had to fight back with something; his presence was making me uncomfortable. He looked good. Adorned in an old UNT sweatshirt and Adidas sweats, I couldn't take my eyes off of him. It was hard not to run into his arms and forgive him for all I thought he'd done, but I had to stay strong. I backed up and stood against the living room wall to give myself leverage and strength.

He walked in closer until we were face-to-face. "I'm just being honest."

"Let's not talk about honesty right now, okay? Especially when yours is in question."

"Why? Why are you questioning my integrity? Have I ever done anything that would cause you not to believe me? You haven't even given me an opportunity to explain."

"Well, start talking because let's face it, with the phone calls, the panties, and the lovely young lady you were so enthralled with on your steps, you need to be saying something. And at this point, whatever you say is going to be pretty difficult to believe. Yeah, you had reasonable explanations for the phone call and the panties, but what the hell are you going to tell me about why you had Alicia all wrapped up in your arms? Please, start talking because I can't wait to hear what you have to say."

He looked away from me and sighed.

"Oh, so now you have nothing to say. Are you nervous, or are you just trying to get your story together? You should have done that shit before you came over here!" I exclaimed disgustedly.

He finally turned around.

"Will you wait one damn minute? I am not nervous, and I am not trying to get my story together. If you want to know the truth, I was praying."

"What?" *I couldn't believe this Negro.*

"I'm praying that you will actually slow down and listen to what I have to say before you fuck up a good relationship."

"What the *hell?* I didn't ask you to come over here. You did that on your own, so if I don't respond like you want me to, then that's just too bad for you. You can take your arrogant ass back home!" Irate, incensed, enraged…I couldn't think of a word to describe how angry I was.

"Arrogant, audacious, presumptuous. I might be all of that, but I am telling the truth. You're about to end this relationship without even knowing all the facts. I know that the circumstantial evidence makes me look extremely guilty, but I am telling you I did not sleep with Alicia. I have never cheated on you."

"Then what the fuck was she doing at your house, and why was she all up in your fucking face like you were ready to make babies?!"

"Look, I know this is going to sound like a load of bullshit but…"

"Well, if you have to preface the statement like that then it probably is bullshit," I spat.

Sampson had remained calm the entire time, but he was reaching his limits. Through clenched teeth he asked, "Would you let me finish, please?"

"Go right ahead, " I said and crossed my arms.

"Alicia is doing all of this on her own. I did not invite her over to my house. She came over on her own. I admit she hit on me, but I wasn't interested. I'm still not interested. When I told her so, she tried to kiss me, but I pushed her away, and that's when you pulled up. If you had taken the time to get out of the car, I could have explained it all right then."

I stood there tapping my foot thinking *Surely, he doesn't expect me to believe this crap,* but instead I responded, "But I didn't get out of the car. So how am I supposed to believe that? Why would I believe that? Do you have any proof? Any evidence?"

He threw his hands up in exasperation. "I knew I was on trial!"

"What the hell is that supposed to mean?"

"Never mind. Listen. Jaslyn, you know I don't have any evidence or proof. But what I hope I do have is your trust. Like I said before, what reason have I ever given you not to trust me? You know me. You know I wouldn't lie to you. You know that if I wanted to see other people, I would have told you. I don't operate in lies. I explained that when I told you about all the women I've been with. I provided you with all the gory specifics about my previous relationships and the type of man I used to be to gain your trust. To let you know I had nothing to hide. But if nothing else, Tamika's messy ass would have said something to you if she had suspected me of anything." He stopped to regain his composure. He deliberated for a few moments, then added, "Don't turn your back on what we have. We have both waited too long and been through too much to let something so stupid ruin what we have together."

He had a point. I debated. The relationships from the past were at the forefront of my mind. After a long pause, I answered him. "I've trusted men before. In the past. It has never worked. Whenever I give my trust, it's misused, and I'm not willing to give it anymore because men abuse it."

I pushed the wrong button. He was finally pissed. "I don't give a shit about no other niggas! I'm not them! Just like you're not any of the women I've ever dated or who've hurt me!" The man must have been a Zen master because he managed to check his anger and return to a state of calm rationality in an instant. He inhaled deeply and continued,

"Don't hold someone else's indiscretions against me. I promise you, I have never cheated on you or lied to you.

"Look, I meant what I said on the phone. I love you, and I know you love me, too. You're the first woman I've been in love with in a long time. Don't allow a simple misunderstanding to ruin our feelings for each other."

My eyes were icy slits. Not because I was angry. I was trying to keep from crying. I bored them into his face trying futilely to hate him. He was wearing me down, but I couldn't allow myself to be put in a position to be hurt again.

"Sam, let me ask you something. If the shoe were on the other foot, would you believe me? Huh?" He didn't say anything. "You know you wouldn't. So, I understand what you're saying about trust and all that, but in this situation, it would be hard to believe anybody, even the man you love. Yeah, you're right, I do love you, but I won't be a fool for anybody. I love you, but I've been too afraid to say anything because it was like what we had was too good to be true. I didn't want to scare you off or fuck it up. I guess I should have said it anyway because it really didn't matter. If you didn't fuck it up, then Alicia sure as hell did."

I sighed. I was tired. Tired of arguing and dealing with all my feelings. Here I was, a therapist, getting paid to help people deal with their feelings, but unable to cope with my own emotional baggage. The irony of it all was too much. "Just go home, Sampson. It was great while it lasted, but I can't risk you hurting me, again."

He pleaded, "Jazz."

"Go home, Sam. Leave before you see a side of me I can never recover from. You know you hate to be yelled at, and right now, I am having a hard time controlling my temper."

I tried to walk around him, but he stepped closer to me. As I tried to escape, he pinned me against the wall. I was breathing hard. My chest rose and fell with the intake of each breath. I was upset and was trying hard to control myself. Deep breathing was the only thing that seemed to help. But in this situation, standing close to him with my back against the wall, the breathing only intensified our emotions. He spoke to me in a low moan, yet, still commanding, "Where are you going? I'm not letting you go anywhere. You hear me. Nowhere." He drew me in his arms and kissed me, his tongue parting my lips.

After all of that bravado and tough talk, he reduced me to a quivering mass in one second. I returned the passion, kissing him urgently as he lifted my t-shirt, and his thumbs caressed my breasts. My nipples sprang to attention. I tried to back away, so he dropped one hand around my waist and pulled me deeper into his embrace. He backed me further against the wall and lifted my hands above my head. With quick motions, he lifted my shirt above my ahead and unzipped my jeans. Before I knew, it they were resting around my ankles. He didn't have to worry about underwear because I didn't put any on after my shower. This morning I was grateful; it would have slowed him down.

My Anthony Hamilton CD started to play. I was floating. On a cloud of sexual ecstasy. He dropped to his knees, and ran his tongue along my stomach. He placed his hands underneath my butt and hoisted one of my legs on his shoulders. His tongue was the hunter, and I was the prey. It entered my body and stayed there to massage my clit. He sucked and licked. A river flowed between my legs, and he did his best to swallow all of me. My feelings were all over the place. I was angry and confused, hurt and disappointed, in love and afraid. Control was no longer an issue. The tears were steady streams flowing down my face. I moaned with desire as my body trembled and shook with gratification. My leg was shaking from the intensity, and I almost couldn't stand straight.

I was finished, but he wasn't. He started licking me again until I was wet once more and ready for more of his loving. He stood and looked me in the eyes. He took his hands and wiped away the tears. He knew I wasn't going anywhere, so he undressed, taking off his sweats, sweat shirt, and shoes. While he stood there completely naked, the tears had reappeared, and he wiped them away for me again. He kissed me then pulled away and whispered in my ear, "All I wanna do is love you, Jaslyn. Let me love you." I looked down at his

long, thick penis as he put on his condom. When he was done
he lifted me off the ground and slid me onto his manhood. He
searched my faced and murmured softly, "Let me love you,
Jaslyn. Just let me love you." His pleas reverberated through
my mind as he started slowly thrusting himself inside me. I
held him tightly around the neck. He moved faster and faster
until his rhythm mirrored mine. Each stroke was a bittersweet
reminder of how much I was in love with him. Every nerve in
my body pulsated, and my skin tingled with the heat of passion.
He drove deeper and deeper within me until the rapture we felt
pierced our souls and he exploded in relief. His body fell limply
against mine. We stood against the wall, holding each other,
panting, and gasping for breath. I dropped my legs and pulled
up my jeans. I put on my shirt while he dressed himself. When
he was done, I looked at him and said, "It's time for you to
go."

Chapter 25
Fucking Nuts

"What the fuck? Time to go? What are you talking about?" Surely, she realized what just happened or was I in some alternate form of hell?

She just stood there with her head down. Tears streaming down her face. "Jaslyn, did you hear me? What the fuck just happened? What was all that about?" I was on the verge of tears myself, and my anger was bubbling over. Then she said it. The most hateful set of words any woman could ever say to me.

She looked up at me and said, "It's called really good break-up sex."

I never wanted to hurt anyone more than I wanted to hurt her right then. Not even when Layla slapped me. My whole spirit sank. *Why was she doing this? Why would she be so willing to hurt me?* I turned and walked out the house before she could see the tears.

Persistence had gotten me nowhere. Here I was pouring my soul out to a woman, and it still didn't matter. Nothing I said or did mattered. So you know what…FUCK JASLYN! She's a god–damned coward. She wants this shit to be easy. Free of worry. No problems. Well, how in the hell does she think we learn to trust? By dealing with our worries and problems, together.

I wish it was easy, but it's not. That's life. In the real world, you deal with your problems. Not run away from them. I know what she's thinking. She thinks that by running away she's avoiding the pain. But she's about to find out what's really painful. Real pain is being in love with someone and not being able to be with them. That's what I feel right now. Pain. And she's about to feel it, too.

Good. Because the shit she did hurt like hell. So, now do you see why I'm through fooling with women? I love this woman, and she loves me. However, we can't be together because of some bullshit.

I can't keep doing this to myself. I'm done. I'll be a bachelor forever, and this time, I mean it. Shit, I might even join a monastery…well, that's going a little too far. Whoever said love could conquer anything LIED. They just flat out lied. I love Jaslyn, and you see where it's gotten me? Nowhere. Who would have ever thought that a misunderstanding would cause a brother so much pain?

I went from never falling in love to giving my whole heart to someone, and the shit backfired. My heart can't take this anymore. Being in love is more work than having a damn job! Shit, I'm going on vacation. A real one. To Bora Bora. Or Pago Pago. Or wherever the hell I can to get my mind off of this woman…shit, women in general. They're driving me FUCKING NUTS! *Shit, shit, shit!*

Epilogue

I bet you forgot all about me, didn't you? Yeah, from the beginning. Well, I'm back. Who am I? It's me, Malik. Throughout the entire story I bet you never guessed that I would be the one to tell it. Not Malik, the misogynistic ex-police officer, wannabe pimp with relationship problems.

I haven't completely reformed but going to jail and losing your job will make you reevaluate all of your priorities and philosophies. Not only that but I was inspired by Jaslyn and Sampson's relationship. I decided it was time to face the truth. We all *want* love. We all *need* love. We just have to be careful how, where, and when we seek love.

What's really important is not the people we end up with, but it's all the work that goes into the previous relationships that count. We go through those trials and tribulations so that when we do find that special someone, we will be able to appreciate them and honor them. Those horrible relationships help us to learn how to be better people for those we really care about. It's called growth.

Sam and Jazz learned. They're still learning. Yes, even Jaslyn. She's just discovering that she needs time to learn more about herself. Let's face it. She was really dealing with infidelities from the past and not Sam's perceived indiscretions. She couldn't trust herself, so how could she trust him?

It's not all bad. Through their turbulent, but brief, relationship, I unearthed an indispensable truth. The labor of love is healing. Moving on from the things that hurt us. My friends had some serious issues from previous hurtful relationships. Neither of them wanted to be stifled by those limitations, and through healing, they found each other. But, the funny thing about healing emotions is that it's a continuous process. They have some more growing to do. They're meant for each other. We can all see that. Maybe one day they'll see it too.

Well, I hope you learned something. I know I did. One day, I'll tell you my story. Now you know there has got to be more to me than Sweet Charlie's.

Acknowledgements

To God, I humbly confess my love. You have placed people and circumstances in my life that made achieving this goal possible. You have shaped and patterned my life in order for me to be right here, right now. Everything I have ever experienced has been in preparation for this moment. I can truly say that I know what Joy feels like, and I understand, now, that I CAN NOT FAIL…no matter how hard I try. Thank You.

To Patricia Kay Cass, my mother. I thank the Lord for you every day. I pray that I honor you, and that I have become someone that you can be proud to call your own. I don't deserve a mother like you, but you always make me feel like I do. Your love for reading and learning sparked a flame in me that will never die. You planted the seed. I hope you like the blossom! To Sarah Cass, my Granny. I love you. Thank you for always telling me, "You can do anything you put your my mind to." I believed you, and you knew that I would. Between you and Mama, I always felt loved.

To my sisters, Michelle, Cassandra, and Adrianne. What can I say? You guys are awesome! I thought you might not understand why I wanted to write a book, but I was amazed to find out that you didn't care why I wanted to write. Y'all just said write the damn thing! Your support for the interviews and questions were tremendous. Thanks for staying on my ass about finishing!

To my father, Julius Castle, I appreciate you now more than ever. Thank you for allowing me to be a part of your life.

To Aunt Joan and my wonderful uncles: Clyde, James, Marvin, Billy, and Wendell "Buck" Cass. You guys are the best. I would never have become the person I am without your guidance. When times are hard you guys can always find the laughter!

To my best friend, Millicent Courtney-Ware, man, we've been to hell and back working and writing together. You are my "George"! Your encouragement, and the friendly competition, was just what I needed to get the job done.

Thanks for reading, re-reading, and stroking my ego on a daily basis...you always seemed to say the right thing just as I was about to give up. We'll lift as we climb! If you make it big, I'm riding your coat tails–you're never getting rid of me. To her husband, Jason, I bet you didn't know I came with the package! Thanks for feeding me, looking out for me, and hooking me up with the music. You two are definitely blessings in my life.

To Oweida and Tangela Carter, my sisters of the heart! Thanks for taking me in and making me your family (or did I force myself on you?). I never would have made it through college (although our nightly games of Tetris and Mortal Combat almost prevented us from graduating), my first job, or my second job without you! Thanks for supporting the book and my dreams. I'm your flaky friend, and you love me for that and I love you for accepting me. Get ready for book two!

Ashley and Bryce Funderburg, I can never say thank you enough for all that you have done to make this book a success. Ashley, I thank God every day that he brought you to Samuell and we became friends, I hope we always remain so; thank you so much for hooking me up with your husband. Bryce your work on the cover is wonderful. You took my mom's concept and turned it into reality. Thanks for allowing me to bug you...and be picky...and be fickle...and make requests at the last minute. I love you both dearly. Thanks!

Jabbar Davis, I almost didn't give you a shout out since, according to you, this book was never going to be written. No, no...I'm just playing. You know I would never forget you. Thanks for being my friend and keeping me on your list; although, I am forever being erased and put back on!

To all my guinea pig friends that allowed me to interview them for this book, I could not have finished without you. Mr. DeMarco King, thanks for being my first interview and for being honest and open. Many thanks go out to Crystal Scott, Candace Carter, Coach Rupert Alexander, Terry Brookins, Byron Maupin, Paul F. Newman, Roy Adams, Donisha Fitts, Alisa Patton, Bruce Pope, and Beverly Turner Cass. To Theo Bowman, a special thanks goes out to you for being the last interview. Thanks for keeping it real and keeping me laughing! I could not have done this without your input. Good looking out.

To William and Katrina Keyes and Carl and Misty Tippen, thanks for providing the married perspective. Your insight on trust and commitment was invaluable. Katrina, thanks for your advice and tips on marketing, and for coming through whenever I call. You constantly tell me how proud you are of me. I hope this time is no different. Misty, since you've known me you have always supported my aspirations as a writer and my love for reading. I can't tell you how much that means to me. Your e-mails of praise were so beautiful I had to save them. Thank you so much! To Donna Houston, thanks for supporting me with your book club and your encouragement. To Tasha Douglas, I hope I give you as much love and encouragement as you have given me. Your prayers mean the world to me, and I appreciate the e-mails to boost me. Please don't stop sending them and don't give up on your book and magazine. They're coming, just keep striving. Remember, God can't fail. I love you, *MAN*!! To Miosha Woods, thanks or supporting me as a teacher and writer. Your editing suggestions were wonderful, and I used *all of them*…but one ☺. Your willingness to invest says so much, and I love you for it. Thank You! To Ms. Kenya Curry, girl you are a blast! I have so much fun with you, and you always keep me in hysterics. Working at Samuell would not have been the same without you, and I'm sure the book signing will be just as entertaining. To Charmeka Calhoun and Kerensa Taylor, your assistance with the cheerleaders was astronomical. You helped relieve some of the stress, which gave me the opportunity to work on this book. I will never forget all you guys have ever done to support me. You all are great sorors, but you're even better friends. Your support means the world to me.

To author J. Monique Gambles, thanks for being a role model. You made the dream tangible. God surrounds you with people for a reason, and I am glad that he sent you to Samuell High School.

My friends, colleagues, and students at W. W. Samuell High School have been a source of inspiration. First, I want to thank Ms. Cheryl Taylor and Anita Carter. Thanks for being my friends and looking out for me from my first day at Samuell. The Samuell book club, Start2Finish: Watina Rayford, Jessie Hall, Karen Vaughn, Sandra Pikes, Marcy Medellin, Ruby Hernandez, Donna Looney, Shenee Davis, and Monica Honorè. A Special thanks goes out to Mrs. Kimberly Jackson-Harris. I can't thank you enough for stepping in and helping me coach the cheerleaders. The last two years were the best! The following students made teaching truly rewarding, and I cannot thank them enough for realizing that my bark was much louder than my actual bite: Nakeisha Calhoun, Benika Ward, Shaniqua Jackson, Chansity Watson, Krystal Stepney, Markeida Barton, I'esah White, Anastasia Watson, Aaron Calhoun, Jr., Christopher Johnson, Bobby Washington, Henderson Boone, Willie Franklin, Christopher Prebble, Martha Ramirez, Tashawanda Derrick, Cindy Paredes, Octavio Ramirez, Juan Cruz, Shellie Choice, Brittany Murphy, Terry Hogan, Luis Monsivais, and Toynisha Monroe. Clyde Pikes, Fred Davis, Eduardo Hernandez, and Willie Henderson, the leadership and mentoring you have provided over the years gave me the courage to be a better me—I love you all.

The graduating class of 1990 Green B. Trimble Technical High School, you know I couldn't mention Dunbar in this book without giving a shout out to the best school in town! What's up, Bulldogs!?

To my brother-in-law, Julian "Dean" Watkins and his friend James Ross. Gee, what can I say about you two? I don't even know where to begin. To tell the truth, you two gave the best interviews! I have never laughed so much in my life and at the same time learned so much about men. Thanks for allowing me to interview you; although, I'm supposed to print your phone numbers so that women can call you. I won't be that crass, but how about this: If you're in Fort Worth and you need a good haircut, you can find Dean at Fine Arts Barbershop in Como, and you can find James Ross cutting hair at Kay's Barbershop on Miller. How is that fellas? (I can't believe I just wrote that! ☺)

Finally, to my nieces and nephews, Jasmine and Adian Watkins and Ashlyn and Jonathon Hall, you guys are the children I will never have! You make me so proud, and I am honored to be your aunt. Words cannot express my love for you. I really do I hope that I make you proud.